The next thing Ben knew, their coffees were ignored and she was in his arms, swaying with him to the soft, slow song.

And this time, when he pulled back and saw the glitter in her eyes, he gave in to the temptation that had been tugging at him all evening and let his mouth brush against hers. Once, very lightly, skimming across her skin.

He felt as if he were going up in flames.

And then her arms tightened around him and she let him deepen the kiss.

He had no idea how long they stayed locked together in the middle of her kitchen, just kissing.

But then reality seeped in.

He hadn't been enough for Karen.

There was no reason why he would be enough for Toni, either.

What was he doing? If this carried on, they were both going to get hurt. Much as he wanted to scoop her up and carry her to her bed, it would be a really reckless, stupid thing to do.

They needed to stop this.

Now.

Dear Reader,

I live about half an hour away from my favorite bit of the world—the North Norfolk coast. Think wide, flat sandy beaches and being able to walk for miles by the sea. Every so often it calls me to write about it, and I merged several of my favorite places to make up "Great Crowmell" (readers of *Reunited at the Altar* will be familiar with it!).

As I live with a much-loved spaniel (who adores going to the beach and galloping around and making a gazillion new friends), it struck me that a dog could be the key to healing someone's heart. So I persuaded my editor to let me include a PAT dog (who is a slightly more sensible version of my own Archie).

Ben comes to Norfolk for a fresh start and Toni's come back to be with her family. Both have been badly hurt and are adamant that they don't want to let their heart get involved again—and both discover that this is the place for second chances...

I hope you enjoy Ben and Toni's story.

With love,

Kate Hardy

A NURSE AND A PUP TO HEAL HIM

—

KATE HARDY

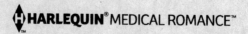

Recycling programs
for this product may
not exist in your area.

ISBN-13: 978-1-335-64167-0

A Nurse and a Pup to Heal Him

First North American Publication 2019

Copyright © 2019 by Pamela Brooks

Printed in U.S.A.

www.Harlequin.com

For Archie—
whose love for the beach inspired this book

CHAPTER ONE

GREAT CROWMELL SURGERY. More than a hundred miles away from his old life in London. Right on the Norfolk coast, a place of wide sands and big skies. Peace. Quiet. No complications. *No lies.* Just him and his new job.

A fresh start.

Ben Mitchell took a deep breath, then pushed the door open.

The receptionist looked up. 'Good morning, Dr Mitchell.'

'Ben, please,' he said with a smile.

'Ben. Welcome to the surgery. The kettle's hot and I made choc-chip cookies yesterday. They're in the staff kitchen. Do help yourself.'

'Thank you, Mrs Hartley.'

'Do call me Moira.' She smiled at him. 'You look like a schoolboy on your first day. Just remember, Ranjit gave you the job because he thought you were the right one for it. You'll be fine.'

Did his nerves really show that much? 'Thank you.' It was ridiculous to feel this nervous. For pity's sake, he'd worked as a GP trainer in London. He was thirty-five. Experienced. He'd done this job for years and years and he knew he was good with patients.

But the first day in a new place would make adrenalin pump through everyone's veins. Having to fit in with an established team; getting to know new people and learn their quirks, their strengths and their weaknesses. Getting to know your patients and working out what they weren't telling you during the consultation so you could help them with their real problem.

Of course he'd be fine. He'd do the job he'd trained to do. The job he loved. Only this time he'd be coming home to a house with no memories and no misery, which made everything a lot easier.

He opened the door with his name on it— *Dr B Mitchell*, in neat capitals—dropped his bag next to his desk and went in search of the staff kitchen to grab a cup of tea and maybe one of Moira's cookies.

But as he turned round the corner he stumbled over a brown and white dog, who yelped and looked sorrowfully up at him with huge amber eyes calculated to extract as much guilt as possible.

'Archie?' The kitchen door opened abruptly. From the dark blue uniform she wore, Ben realised that this must be one of the practice nurses, probably the one the senior partner had mentioned being on leave when Ben had come for his interview and met the rest of the team. What was her name? Terry?

She frowned at him and bent down to stroke the dog, who whined softly. 'What happened?'

'I didn't see the dog and I tripped over it.'

'Him,' she corrected, her eyes narrowing. Beautiful grey eyes, like the sky in November. It shocked him that he'd actually noticed.

'I'm sorry,' he said, knowing that he was in the wrong for hurting the dog, albeit completely unintentionally. But at the same time nobody would expect to find a dog in the corridor in a family doctor's surgery. 'I didn't mean to hurt the dog. But it shouldn't be here. What if it bit a patient?'

'*He*,' she corrected again, 'barely even

nipped when he was a puppy. He's incredibly gentle.'

'There's always a first time,' he said crisply, 'and our patients' health and safety have to come first.'

The look she gave him said very clearly, *You're throwing your weight around this much on your first day here?* 'It does indeed,' she said, surprising him, as he'd expected her to make some kind of protest.

She wasn't smiling when she added, 'Though our patients happen to like having Archie around on Mondays. As do the rest of the staff. And there's an infection control policy in the surgery.'

On Mondays? Why was the dog specifically here on Mondays? But, before he could ask her, she clicked her fingers and the dog got up and trotted behind her to the door next to his, which she closed a little too loudly behind them.

Nurse Practitioner Toni Butler.

Toni. He'd remembered a masculine-sounding name. Short for Antonia? Not that it mattered.

He'd just got off to a really bad start with one of his new colleagues.

But he stood by his view that a dog had no

place in a family doctor's surgery, regardless of an infection control policy being in place. Some patients were frightened of dogs; others were allergic and the dander from the dog's fur could trigger an asthma attack in a vulnerable patient.

Nobody said a word about the little spat when he walked into the kitchen, but he was pretty sure from the awkwardness in everyone's faces that they'd all overheard the conversation. He felt embarrassed enough to do nothing more than mumble a brief hello and go straight into his consulting room without bothering to make himself a mug of tea.

At least his patients all seemed pleased to see him during the morning's surgery, welcoming him to the village. He settled into the routine of talking to his patients and suggesting self-help measures as well as medication.

At lunchtime, Toni and the dog were nowhere to be seen.

'How was your first morning?' Moira asked.

Apart from having a fight with the nurse practitioner over her dog? 'Fine, thanks,' he said.

'Good. If you haven't brought anything with you for lunch, there are a few cafés plus the deli and the fish and chip shop along the harbour front—and of course Scott's do the best ice cream in the area. Abby Scott—well, Powell, since she got remarried to Brad—has even developed a special ice cream for dogs. Toni's one of her most loyal customers.'

'Ice cream for dogs?' He'd never heard of such a thing.

'Archie loves it.' Moira smiled. 'Everyone loves Archie.'

Pretty much what Toni had said to him. In his view, the dog still had no place in a doctor's surgery; though Ben rather thought he'd be on a losing wicket if he protested any further.

'Hello, Ginny.' Toni kissed the elderly woman's papery cheek and sat down next to her. 'How are you today?'

Ginny didn't answer. She hadn't said a word in three months, now. Given that her dementia was advanced, she'd either forgotten what to say or she couldn't quite piece together what Toni was saying enough to answer her. But she smiled, and her smile brightened even more when she saw Archie.

This was exactly why Toni had trained her spaniel as a therapy dog. A dog could sometimes get through to someone when a human couldn't, and could bring a spot of brightness into a sick person's day. Residents at a nursing home had often had to leave a much-loved pet behind, and the chance to relive happy memories was so good for them. When Toni's grandmother had been in the nursing home, a visitor with a dog had really helped brighten her mood. Toni desperately wanted to give something back— to help someone the way her grandmother had been helped. And Ginny had been one of her grandmother's best friends and who'd been like a second grandmother to Toni and Stacey when they'd been growing up; Toni desperately wanted to make a difference to Ginny's last days.

Archie, once his fluorescent coat was on, went into work mode, being gentle and sweet and sitting perfectly still to let an elderly patient or a young child pet him, suppressing his natural instinct to bounce everywhere. At the nursing home, Toni came to the lounge so all the residents could spend a few minutes with the dog in turn, and it also meant that one of the staff would be present at all times, in accordance with therapy dog visiting rules.

'Hey, Toni. Hello, Archie, you gorgeous boy.' Julia, the nursing home manager, came over to them and scratched behind the dog's ears. 'Look, Ginny, it's your favourite visitor.'

Ginny didn't reply, but she smiled.

'Catch me in my office on the way out, Toni?' Julia asked quietly.

'Sure.' Toni knew it was Julia's way of saying that she wanted to talk to her privately about a couple of potential health complications among the residents.

'Thanks.' Julia patted her shoulder.

Toni spent a few more minutes with Ginny, letting her stroke the dog and hopefully latch on to happy memories of dogs in her past, then said gently, 'Ginny, Archie needs to go and visit Ella now. We'll come back and see you next week. Say "bye", Arch.'

The dog gave a quiet 'woof'.

Toni did her usual round in the lounge, chatting with the residents in turn and letting them make a fuss of the dog. At the end of her allotted two hours—the maximum length of time for a therapy dog session—she made a fuss of Archie, said goodbye to the residents and headed for Julia's office.

The nursing home manager nodded at her

drawer, where Toni knew she kept a box of dog treats especially for Archie. 'May I?'

'Sure. He's earned it—plus we're going for a run on the beach when we leave here, so we'll burn it off,' she said with a smile.

Archie, knowing from long experience what was coming, sat beautifully and offered a paw.

Julia grinned, rubbed the top of his head and gave him a treat. 'I love the fact you visit us on Mondays. It really sets our residents up for the week, not to mention the staff.'

'He loves it, too,' Toni said. 'I assume you wanted to talk to me about a couple of residents?'

'Yes.' Julia took three files out of her drawer. 'I think Liza is brewing a UTI. I did a dipstick test this morning, and although it wasn't conclusive I'd like to nip any infection in the bud before it becomes full-blown.'

Toni knew that urinary tract infections could cause additional confusion in elderly patients, making dementia worse; and they were more frequent in elderly patients who sometimes refused to drink enough and weren't that mobile. 'OK. Do another dipstick test in the morning and let me know the results. I'll flag it up at the team meeting tomorrow and see what everyone's schedule looks like. Either I'll come out tomorrow myself and see them, or I'll get one of the doctors to come out; we won't wait until our scheduled weekly visit on Thursday.' Toni checked the notes. 'This is potentially her fourth UTI in three months, so I'd like to look at giving her a lower dose of antibiotics long-term as prophylaxis.' As a nurse practitioner, Toni was able to prescribe antibiotics rather than having to consult one of the GPs, which made life a lot easier.

'Agreed.' Julia, as the nursing home manager, was also a qualified geriatric nurse and Toni knew she was good at picking up early signs. 'And I'm also a bit concerned about Renée. I've noticed she has a bit of a tremor when she holds a mug, and she's been a little bit off with everyone for the last couple of days.'

'You think her lithium levels might need rebalancing?' Toni asked, knowing that Renée was bipolar; lithium levels in Renée's blood needed to be checked regularly, to make sure they weren't too high and the drug was doing its job properly. A tremor was often one of the first signs of a problem, along with a change in mood.

Julia nodded. 'Again, I'd like to catch it early if we can.'

'I'll take a blood sample now and drop it in to the surgery on my way back,' Toni said. 'We've missed the bloods pick-up for today, but I'll pop the sample in the fridge overnight and it'll go in tomorrow's batch. We'll ring you as soon as the results are through.'

'Thank you.'

She washed her hands, and went to see the charge nurse to pick up a syringe, a plaster, a phial and a label. Renée was a little more scattered than usual and kept wringing her hands. 'They don't like me in here, you know,' she confided. 'They're going to tell me to leave.'

Toni knew from experience that when Renée was worried, she'd keep circling back to the same fears and no reassurance would work for longer than a couple of minutes; it just needed a couple of days for her lithium levels to get back in balance and her mood would change and her worries would disappear. So instead Toni gently asked if Renée would mind her taking a blood sample, then after her agreement changed the subject to the weather and how pretty the sunset had been last night.

Thankfully, the distraction worked and she was able to take the sample, then reassured Renée a little more before going to see Julia again to collect Archie.

'Even before we get the test results, from her behaviour I'm pretty sure you're right and her lithium levels are out of balance,' she said. 'But we need the numbers to fine-tune the dosage, and although I can prescribe a few things this is a medication I'll have to talk to one of the GPs about.'

'OK. Until we get the results back, we'll keep reassuring her and changing the subject so she doesn't get too anxious,' Julia said. 'Thanks, Toni. It's appreciated.'

'No problem. One of us will come out to see you tomorrow,' Toni said, 'and Archie and I will see you next Monday afternoon.'

'She's a smashing girl, Toni,' Mr Fellowes said. 'She used to work in a big London hospital. We're lucky to have her.'

The nurse practitioner had come here from London, too? And it was unusual to move from a hospital to a general practice. Had she been burned out, in London? Ben wondered. Or had there been some other reason why she'd come here? Even though they'd

clashed, Ben had been very aware of her—
and, despite his intentions never to get involved with anyone again, he found that she
intrigued him.

Mr Fellowes went on to answer the un-
spoken question. 'She came home to help
her sister look after their grandmother when
she became ill. Lovely woman, Betty Butler.
Her girls did her proud.'

Which sounded as if Toni and her sister
had been brought up by their grandmother.
Which was none of his business, Ben reminded himself. He wasn't going to ask
what had happened to her parents, or why
her grandmother had needed looking after,
or if her grandmother was still around. It was
nothing to do with him.

'She'd do anything to help anyone, our
Toni.'

Which told him that the nurse practitioner
was kind as well as being popular. He felt
another twinge of guilt. Maybe he'd overreacted a bit about the dog. Or maybe he'd
overreacted because he'd noticed the colour
of her eyes and his awareness of her had
spooked him slightly because he hadn't noticed small details like that about anyone for
the last two years.

'That's good to know,' he said neutrally, and guided the conversation back to the ulcer on Mr Fellowes' lower leg that refused to heal.

Toni dropped the blood sample into the surgery. She wasn't sure if she was more relieved or disappointed not to see the new GP again, which unsettled her slightly. If he was a hotshot London doctor like Sean had been, he was the last person she wanted to spend time around. And yet there was something about him that drew her.

She shook herself, and drove to the car park by the beach. She changed into her running shoes, slung a bag over her shoulder with two bottles of water and a bowl for the dog, then clipped his lead on and took him to the dog-friendly side of the beach before letting him off the lead again so he could bound along the sand.

The tide was halfway out; she followed the dog down to the shoreline, enjoying the freshness of the slight breeze coming off the sea and the swishing sound of the waves against the sand. Running produced the usual endorphins; by the time they'd run along the shore and then back to the car park, she was feeling much less grumpy than she had after her run-in with Ben Mitchell.

She picked up a home-made apple pie at the beach café and a sausage for Archie, then clipped the dog into his harness on the back seat and drove to her sister's house.

Stacey greeted her with a hug. 'Perfect timing. The kettle's hot.'

'Lovely. I'm dying for a mug of tea. And I brought pudding.' Toni kissed her sister and handed over the apple pie. 'How's my best niece?' she asked, lifting Scarlett out of her bouncy chair and giving her a cuddle.

Scarlett giggled and plastered a mushy kiss to Toni's cheek. 'Tee-to!'

Scarlett-speak for Auntie Toni; Toni was so glad she'd stayed in Norfolk and had the chance to watch her niece grow up instead of going back to London, when maybe she would only have seen her sister once a month and missed all the important milestones in her niece's development.

'How's your day been, Stace?' Toni asked.

'Good. We had toddler group this morning, and Mary brought her guitar in. Then we went for a picnic in the park. How about you?'

'My usual Monday afternoon at The

Beeches,' Toni said. 'Archie brought a smile to a few faces.'

'That's good. Though it must be bitter-sweet for you, going back and knowing Gran isn't there any more,' Stacey said softly.

Toni nodded. 'It is. And I know you miss her, too.' There was a lump in her throat. 'She would've adored Scarlett.' Except Betty Butler had died from pneumonia, the month before Scarlett was born. In some ways Toni had been relieved, because at last her grand-mother was out of pain and confusion; but in others she'd been devastated. Another link to the past severed. If only Betty hadn't devel-oped dementia. If only their parents hadn't died. They would all have loved Scarlett so much. And it must be even harder for her sister with all the might-have-beens.

'Yes.'

Hearing the slight crack in her sister's voice and knowing they were sharing the same regrets, Toni changed the subject. 'The new doctor started at the practice today.'

'What's he like?'

Toni wrinkled her nose. 'Your age, I'd say. Tall, dark and grumpy.'

'Not handsome?'

'I didn't notice.' It was a slight fib. Ben

Mitchell was very nice-looking. Or he would be if he actually smiled. And his eyes were the same green as the sea on a spring day. Not that she should be focusing on that.

'But *grumpy*?' Stacey shook her head. 'I can't imagine Ranjit offering a place to someone grumpy. Someone like that just wouldn't fit in at the practice.'

Ranjit Sidana, the head of the practice at Great Crowmell, was one of the nicest-natured men either of them had ever met, always full of smiles.

'We clashed a bit.' Toni rolled her eyes. 'Over Archie. He didn't approve of the dog being at the surgery.'

'Maybe it was first-day nerves,' Stacey suggested. 'You know what Gran would've said. Give him time to settle in before you judge him.'

'I guess.'

'So what do you know about him? Is he married? Single? Any children?'

Toni heard the hopeful note in her sister's voice and sighed inwardly. 'I have absolutely no idea. All Ranjit told us about him was that he's moved here from London.'

'Like you did.'

'From another practice, rather than a hospital.' And the reason why he'd moved from the capital to a quiet country practice was none of her business. 'Even if he isn't involved with someone, I'm really not interested, Stacey. You don't have to hope that he's a potential date for me. I don't want to date anyone.'

Stacey squeezed her shoulder. 'You know I worry about you being alone.'

'I'm not alone. I live in the same village as the best sister and brother-in-law and niece in the world, I have plenty of friends locally, and I have Archie to keep me company at home.'

Stacey raised an eyebrow. 'Thank you for the compliment, but you know what I meant. Surely you'd like to share your life with someone who says more than just "woof"?'

Toni laughed. 'There's an awful lot to be said for talking to someone who doesn't answer back.'

As if to emphasise her point, Archie wagged his tail and licked Stacey's hand and then Scarlett's foot, making the little girl giggle.

'I swear you trained him to do that on purpose.' But Stacey was smiling. 'Just don't let

Sean the Smug put you off finding happiness with someone else. Not all men are like him.'

'I know they're not.' But she hadn't managed to pick anyone who felt right before him, either. 'I'm doing just fine on my own, Stacey. I live in my favourite place in the world, I love my job, and I have my family and friends nearby. I don't need anything else.'

'Hint taken, and I'll stop nagging,' Stacey said.

For now, Toni thought. She knew her sister's motives were good, but her life really was just fine as it was. Toni felt very much part of the village where she'd grown up and she had absolutely no regrets about coming here from London. She had a great life; she didn't need to date someone.

She didn't need to prove her judgement to herself, either. Of course she knew that not all men were as selfish and demanding as her ex. But if she was honest with herself she knew that the two men she'd dated before him had been just as single-minded and just as selfish as Sean. Sometimes she wondered if she subconsciously picked men who just couldn't give her love and security so it wouldn't break her heart when things went wrong. She'd already lost too many people who really mattered at too young an age. Sean had given her an ultimatum: dump her grandmother, or be dumped. That one had been very easy, and she was done with ultimatums.

Single and happy. That was her. And that was the way she intended to stay.

'Let's get you back down in your chair, Miss Beautiful,' she said to her niece, 'and I'm going to help your mummy cook dinner.'

'Din-dins,' Scarlett said, and beamed.

CHAPTER TWO

On Tuesday morning, Ben was in early for the weekly team meeting. 'I made brownies,' he said, taking the lid off the tin and putting it in the centre of the table.

'Thank you. Good choice,' Ranjit, the head of the practice, said with a smile.

Everyone except Toni took a brownie; Ben sighed inwardly. Obviously he'd annoyed her enough that she was going to ignore his peace offering. Well, he'd had it with women who were snippy. He'd put up with it from Karen—until he'd learned the bitter truth—and he wasn't going to bend over backwards to please Toni Butler.

Once they'd gone through the morning's agenda, Ranjit asked, 'Is there anything that anyone wants to bring up?'

'Yes—we need someone out at The Beeches today, please,' Toni said. She looked at Ben. 'That's the local nursing home. Forty beds; and they're set up for patients with dementia. We need to follow up Liza's UTI and Renée's lithium levels.'

'Can you do the follow-up for us, Ben?' Ranjit asked. 'It'd be useful for you to meet Julia and her team.'

'Sure.' He looked at Toni. 'Do you do a regular practice visit, Nurse Practitioner Butler?'

'Toni,' she said.

Oh. So she was thawing slightly. Good. He wouldn't go out of his way to make friends with her, but a decent working relationship would be good both for the team and for their patients.

'Our practice's regular visit is on Thursdays, though obviously we pop in whenever we're needed as well.' Her grey eyes were very clear. 'I visit The Beeches on my Monday afternoons off with Archie. He's a therapy dog. I bring him to the surgery with me on Monday morning because I go straight from here to the nursing home.'

'A therapy dog.' He hadn't expected that.

'No doubt you disapprove of that, too,' she said.

He blew out a breath. Maybe he'd asked

for that, because he'd reacted badly to the dog yesterday. But she'd been snippy with him, too. 'No. I've seen studies showing that having a pet visiting can really help elderly people, especially those in residential care.'

'Exactly. It helps the residents—even a small observational study by the manager at The Beeches last year showed that a visit from Archie helps with the residents' moods and helps with their social interaction with the staff as well as each other. It gives the residents something to talk about other than their illness, and even the ones who don't really hold a conversation any more smile when they see him. The residents all really look forward to Mondays. And obviously it's done in a supervised environment, we know that none of the residents is allergic or afraid of dogs, and we're very aware of infection control. There's a policy at the home as well as here.'

She'd just covered everything he'd brought up yesterday. Clearly what he'd said still rankled. He knew what he needed to do. 'I apologise,' he said, 'for snapping at you yesterday.'

She inclined her head in acknowledgement. 'But you don't like dogs.'

Now she'd brought it up… 'No. Obviously I'd never hurt one, but I wouldn't go out of my way to spend time with one.'

'I get that not everyone's a dog person,' Toni said. 'But Archie is a genuinely nice dog. He's passed a very thorough assessment—he can be stroked and handled by anyone and he'll take treats gently and wait patiently. Plus he doesn't jump up, paw people or lick them too much.'

And Ben could guess exactly why that was part of the assessment. 'Because elderly people have very frail, thin skin.'

She smiled at him, then. A genuine smile. And Ben was shocked to realise that it made him feel as if the room had just lit up. This wasn't good. He didn't want to be attracted to anyone. His life was on an even keel again and he wanted it to stay that way.

He needed to keep his thoughts on his job. 'All right. I'll go to the home at lunchtime, as soon as my surgery finishes,' he promised.

'Thank you.'

Now she was smiling rather than scowling at him, Toni Butler was seriously pretty. She didn't wear a ring on her left hand, but that meant nothing; she could still be in a serious relationship with someone without being married. He wasn't going to ask and start the gossip mill working, either. She was his colleague. End of. And, even if she was single, he'd learned his lesson the hard way. Relationships were just too fragile, too easily broken. Like his heart. He'd only just finished putting himself back together after Karen and Patrick's betrayal, and he had no intention of setting himself up for a repeat of all that heartache.

Toni was always a little bit suspicious of people who didn't like dogs. She didn't understand that mindset. But she knew she hadn't really given Ben Mitchell a chance; she'd let herself react to him as if he was like Sean, expecting her to do things his way with no discussion, so she'd been combative with him rather than trying to find common ground, the way she normally would.

Of course not all men were like her ex.

But Ben was as self-assured as Sean had been, something that instinctively made her wary. Plus he was the first man since Sean who'd made her look twice. When he'd smiled back at her in the staff meeting and lost that brooding look, he'd been breathtakingly beautiful—green eyes, dark hair that flopped over his forehead, and an incredibly sensual mouth. He could have rivalled any film star. She really hadn't expected to be so attracted to him.

But she knew that romantic relationships never worked out for her, so she had no intention of acting on that attraction. A good working relationship was all they needed. End of.

After his shift, Ben tapped the address of The Beeches into his satnav and headed out to see the patients.

When he introduced himself to Julia, the manager, she said, 'Ah, yes. You must be the new doctor at the practice. How are you settling in?'

'Fine, thanks. Nurse Butler said you had a patient who needed to be seen about a possible UTI, and it made sense for me to come and introduce myself because I'll be seeing you on some of the regular Thursday morning visits,' he said.

'Good call. Thank you.' She smiled at him.

'I'd also like to say hello to Renée, even though her blood test results aren't back yet,' he said.

'Of course. Toni's filled you in on all the patients' histories?'

Yes, but it was useful to go over it again in case he'd missed anything. 'I'm happy for you to tell me whatever you think I need to know,' Ben said.

After he'd seen the two patients Toni had been worried about, Ben made time to meet the charge nurse, who was responsible for the drug round, and introduced himself to all the residents who were in the lounge.

'I agree with you about Renée. We'll review her medication as soon as her bloods are back and ring you,' he said to Julia in her office at the end of his visit. 'And I agree with Toni that we should give Liza a low dose of antibiotics for the next six months to put a stop to the UTIs. I'll get the prescriptions sorted out so they'll be ready for collection later this afternoon.'

'Thank you,' Julia said. 'Nice to meet you, Dr Mitchell.'

'Ben,' he said with a smile.

Once he'd sorted out the prescriptions and some admin back at the surgery, he headed for the supermarket on the way home to pick up a couple of pints of milk. As he walked into the chiller aisle, he saw Toni putting a bottle of milk into her trolley.

'Hello,' he said.

'Hi.'

No dog, he noticed. But of course dogs weren't usually allowed in supermarkets, so he stopped himself asking something clueless. Instead, he opted for polite small talk. 'Doing your weekly grocery shop?'

'My neighbour's, actually,' she said. 'Shona came off her bike awkwardly three weeks ago and broke her arm.'

'That's kind of you to do her shopping.'

Toni shrugged. 'She'd do the same for me. Great Crowmell is the kind of place where people look out for each other.' She smiled. 'Right now she has Archie sprawled all over her lap, enjoying having a fuss made of him.'

The dog. She was very much a dog person, and he really wasn't. 'Uh-huh.'

She bit her lip. 'You and I rather got off on the wrong foot yesterday. Look, if you're not busy this evening, why don't you come over for dinner? I'm a reasonable cook.'

Awareness flickered through him, and he stifled it. She wasn't asking him to dinner because she was attracted to him. She was asking him because she was trying to get their professional relationship onto an even keel. Which would be a good thing, and he'd accept purely on that basis. Because he really wasn't interested in starting a relationship with anyone. Karen had hurt him deeply. He wasn't letting anyone that close again, even if Toni was as nice as she seemed. 'Thanks. Dinner would be great,' he said.

'You're welcome to bring your partner, too, and any children,' she said. 'Just let me know how many I'm cooking for.'

Partner and children. Not any more. It had left a huge hole in his life that he tried to fill with work and studying. It hadn't worked, which was why he had moved here, hoping that a fresh start would help. He pushed the thought away. 'Just me.'

'It's just me and Archie at my place.'

So she was single, too—and clearly not in the market for a relationship. He was glad that they'd cleared that up. Established boundaries. 'OK. Can I bring pudding?' Then he remembered her refusal of his brownies. 'Um—that is, do you eat pudding?'

She grimaced. 'Ah. You must've noticed I didn't take one of your brownies this morning. Sorry, it wasn't anything personal.' She gave him a rueful smile. 'My sister says I'm weird, because I'm about the only person in the world who doesn't actually like chocolate cake.'

Funny how that made him feel so much better to discover that she hadn't been snippy with him; she just didn't like brownies. 'Noted. And I'll make blondies, next time,' he said.

'Thank you. And yes, please to pudding.'

'As long as it's not chocolate,' he confirmed.

'Absolutely. Is there anything you're allergic to or don't eat?'

'Allergies? Spoken like a true medic.' He couldn't help smiling back at her. 'No allergies, and I eat anything.'

'Good. I'll see you tonight then. About seven?'

'I'll be there.'

She gave him her address. 'It's on the edge of town, but there's plenty of parking in my road.'

'You're not that far from me. A walk will do me good,' he said. 'See you at seven.'

* * *

Sean had always said she was too impulsive.

Maybe he had a point, Toni thought as she finished buying Shona's groceries. But she was going to have to work with Ben Mitchell. It made sense to make sure their working relationship was a good one, for their patients' sake. But she was feeling ever so slightly guilty about being judgemental towards him yesterday. OK, so he'd annoyed her with his attitude towards Archie; but she could almost hear her grandmother saying softly, 'Walk a mile in someone else's shoes before you judge them.'

She hadn't done that at all.

So the very least she could do was to cook dinner for the man and help him settle into the community.

She bought ingredients for dinner, dropped off Shona's groceries and put them away for her, and took Archie out for a run before making a start on dinner.

At precisely seven o'clock, her doorbell rang.

Ben stood there with an armful of gifts. 'I bought a lemon tart and raspberries for pudding. I hope that's OK.'

'Perfect, thank you—I'm baking salmon

with pesto, so the lemon will pick up the basil,' she said with a smile.

'I forgot to ask if you prefer red or white wine, so I've played it safe.' He handed her a bottle of wine.

'Lovely. New Zealand Sauvignon blanc is my favourite,' she said.

'And—well, I was brought up to take flowers if someone invites you to dinner,' he said.

'Thank you. They're beautiful,' she said, accepting the sunflowers. 'Come through to the kitchen and I'll pop them in water and sort out a drink.'

'Thanks.'

'I should warn you that Archie's in the kitchen. But if you'd prefer me to put him in the garden while you're here, I will.'

Toni was clearly trying to make an effort to accommodate him, Ben thought. So maybe he needed to do the same. 'It's fine. Though I didn't grow up around dogs and I don't have a clue how to behave around them, so you'll have to give me some pointers.'

He knew he'd done the right thing by the way she smiled at him—the real full wattage instead of the polite and more subdued version, and it lit up her eyes, too; it made his heart miss a beat.

'Thank you. Come and say hello.' She ushered him into the kitchen, where Archie sat in his basket, wagging his tail and clearly desperate to bounce over and greet their visitor, but at a signal from Toni he stayed exactly where he was.

'He's very well trained,' Ben commented.

'He is,' she agreed. 'And he'll stay there until I tell him he can come and say hello to you. If you feel uncomfortable, just let me know. Springers are usually pretty bouncy and exuberant—and Archie is definitely springy when he gets the chance— but they're also very kind, biddable dogs who just love to be with people.' She looked at him. 'If you hold your hand out to him, he'll sniff you, and then you can stroke the top of his head. As a therapy dog, he's used to elderly people with thin skin, and being around very young children who might be nervous or unpredictable. So he's very, very gentle.'

'You work with children as well?' Ben asked, surprised.

'I go into the school on Wednesday mornings,' she said. 'We're there to help the reluctant readers, the ones who are too nervous to read out loud in front of the class. They come and read to Archie.' She grinned. 'The head teacher thought it was a completely bonkers idea at first, when I suggested it.'

Yup. He thought it was bonkers, too. But the passion in her eyes as she talked about her work drew him.

'But we've seen the shyest and most hesitant little ones really grow in confidence since they've been reading to Archie. They all improved their reading ages by several months in the first six weeks alone.' She smiled. 'As a reward for good behaviour, two of the children get to sort out his water bowl and mat. They love doing that, so it's a really strong motivator.'

'Reading to dogs.' He shook his head in amazement. 'I had no idea that was even a thing.'

'There are quite a few schemes with therapy dogs,' she said. 'Archie loves it, and so do the kids. If he falls asleep, I tell them it's not because he's bored—it's like when someone reads them a bedtime story and they go all relaxed and sleepy.'

Ben was beginning to see what made Toni Butler tick. His patients and his colleagues had all sung her praises; now he could see why.

'OK.' He took a deep breath. 'I'll stroke him.'

'Stay, Archie,' she said softly.

The dog stayed where he was and let Ben stroke the top of his head. Exactly what Toni had promised: Archie was a sweet, kind, biddable dog with soft, soft fur and big, soulful amber eyes.

'Studies show,' she said, 'that blood pressure goes down when someone pets a dog. And in times of stress dog-owners experience less cardiovascular reactivity.' She looked rueful. 'Though I'm guessing if you're not a dog person...'

'It's probably still the same,' he said.

'Dinner is in five minutes. Would you like a glass of wine?'

'That'd be lovely,' he said.

Her kitchen was very neat and tidy; and there were photographs held to the door of her fridge with magnets, of herself and Archie with various groups of people, all smiling. It was clear that she led a full and happy life.

Dinner was scrumptious: salmon baked with pesto, new potatoes, asparagus, baby carrots and roasted courgettes. Karen hadn't been keen on cooking; and Ben hadn't bothered much since his marriage had broken up because cooking for one was so lonely. He'd almost forgotten what it was like to share a meal with someone, except when his parents and his sister had invited him over and then tried to matchmake because they wanted him to be happy again.

But this was his new beginning. He and Toni could be friends as well as colleagues. He damped down the burgeoning thought that maybe she could be more.

'This is really lovely,' he said.

'And—apart from the salmon, obviously, and the pine nuts in the pesto—everything is homegrown. I love June because the garden's just brilliant.'

'You're a gardener?' He hadn't expected that.

'Not as good as my grandmother was. But that's why I moved here rather than to one of the fisherman's cottages near the harbour— it means I have a garden for Archie, and I've got space for a small vegetable patch. I got my brother-in-law to haul some railway sleepers for me to make raised beds.'

'So have you been here for very long?'

'At this cottage, for two years. But I grew up in Great Crowmell,' she said. 'My parents died in a car crash when I was twelve and my sister Stacey was fourteen, and Gran swept us up and brought us to live with her. Before that, we used to stay with her every summer. We'd spend whole days on the beach and thought we were in paradise. We lived in London, and that tiny bit of sand you get on the banks of the Thames every so often just wasn't enough for us. We loved it here, where the sand went on for miles.'

'You grew up in London?' He looked at her in surprise.

'In Highgate, when my parents were still alive. Then, when I trained as a nurse, I lived in Victoria and worked in the emergency department of the London Victoria hospital.'

'So you went back to the bright lights?'

'Something like that.'

'So what made you come back?' He knew the question was intrusive as soon as it was out of his mouth, because she flinched. 'Sorry. You don't have to answer that.' And then maybe she wouldn't ask him why he'd moved, either.

'No, it's fine. I came back because Gran became ill.' She looked at him. 'She had dementia. Stacey went to college here and stayed after she finished—she's a dress-maker—but it wasn't fair to leave all the looking-after to her, so I came back to sup-port them both. I found a job at the practice, and I moved in with Gran so she didn't have to go into residential care for a few more months.' She shrugged. 'Gran didn't hesitate when we needed her, and we didn't hesitate when she needed us. I just wish she'd been here to meet Scarlett—my niece. She's four-teen months old.'

Now Ben understood why Toni's life had undergone such a sea change, why she'd switched from working in a big London hospital to this small general practice in the country. 'You never wanted to go back to London after your grandmother died?'

She shook her head. 'I love the pace of emergency medicine and knowing that you can make such a huge difference to people's lives, and I always thought I'd go back to it after Gran died. But then I discovered that actually I like working in the practice more than I do at a hospital. It's cradle to grave medicine. You know your patients, you can watch the little ones grow up and blossom, and because you know their family history you've got a lot more chance of working out what your patient feels too awkward to tell you in a consultation. Plus my family is here—and I really missed Stacey when I was in London.'

There was a slight shadow in her eyes; or maybe he'd misread it, because it was gone again within an instant. He had a feeling that there was another reason why she hadn't gone back to London after her grandmother's death, but he wasn't going to pry. It was none of his business. Plus asking her would leave himself open to questions, and he didn't want to talk about Karen and Patrick.

'That's why I chose to be a GP rather work in a hospital,' Ben said. 'I like working in a community.'

'Where were you before here?' she asked.

'London. Chalk Farm. We lived not far from Primrose Hill, so I was lucky enough to be able to do my morning run in the park there—the view of the city is amazing.'

'It sounds as if you miss it.'

'I do.' But he didn't miss the misery that

had dragged through the last few months of his marriage, or the two years of loneliness since. He'd put it down to pregnancy hormones and he'd tried his best to be supportive and understanding. And then, just before the twenty-week scan, Karen had dropped the final bombshell; and he'd realised that the reason they hadn't been getting on was nothing to do with hormones and everything to do with guilt...

'There are good places to run, here. And if it's low tide you really can't beat running by the edge of the sea. If you're lucky, you might even see some seals,' she said. 'Why did you move here from London?'

The question he'd dreaded: though it was the obvious one and he should've found an anodyne answer for it by now. Except there wasn't one.

Because my wife fell in love with my best friend and broke my heart along with our marriage. Not that he wanted to discuss that. It had taken him nearly two years to get past it, and he didn't want to dwell on it now.

'Do you have family in the area?' she asked.

'No. Sometimes you just need a change,'

he said. 'This seemed like a nice place to live.'

And the best way to distract Toni from asking anything else, he thought, would be to switch the conversation back to her dog. 'So what made you decide to train Archie as a therapy dog?'

'When Gran went into the nursing home, one of the other residents used to be visited by her dog, and seeing the dog always made Gran's day brighter. After she went into the home, I got Archie to keep me company. The manager at the care home suggested training him as a therapy dog and bringing him to The Beeches. I looked into it, and I think we both enjoy it.'

'That's good.' He kept the conversation neutral until pudding.

'Oh, now this is sublime. Thank you so much.' She ate the lemon tart with relish. 'Lemony puddings are the best—and it's the perfect pairing with raspberries.'

'Agreed.' He couldn't help smiling. 'So you're a foodie?'

'Guilty as charged,' she said, smiling back. 'I'm really interested in nutrition, and because I'm in charge of the diabetic patients I was thinking about trying to do something to teach them to tweak their favourite dishes to make them diabetic-friendly. And I'd quite like to do the same for our cardiac patients. So maybe I could run a cookery class or maybe develop a section on the practice website to help with meal plans and recipes.'

'That sounds good. The diet and exercise routines that work best are the ones you enjoy, because you stick to them,' he said.

'I've already gathered that you're a foodie, too; do I take it from the brownies that you're a cook as well?' she asked.

'I'm reasonable,' he said. Karen had left all the cooking to him, and he'd enjoyed it, finding it relaxing. Though he hadn't bothered much since she'd left him for Patrick. Cooking for one felt too lonely, and the brownies were the first cakes he'd made in months.

'Maybe we can work together on the project?' she suggested.

The previous day, Ben had disliked Toni and he hadn't been able to work out why everyone else seem to adore her. Now, he could see exactly why they did. Her warmth, her bright ideas, the way she tried to include everyone.

If he was honest with himself, he was attracted to her as well as liking her. But he had no intention of acting on that attraction. He wasn't setting himself up for things to go wrong again.

But colleagues and friends—he could do that. With pleasure.

'I'd like that,' he said. 'Do we have regular clinics for our diabetic and cardiac patients?'

'Diabetics, yes—that's me on Thursday mornings,' she said.

'It might be worth asking them for suggestions of dishes they'd like us to help them tweak. And maybe we could look at regular clinics for our cardiac patients and do the same with them.'

'Great idea.' She smiled at him. 'I'll work up a proposal, we can fine-tune it together, and then we can talk Ranjit into it.'

'Deal.'

Shaking her hand was a mistake. Awareness of her prickled all the way through him. He was going to have to be very careful to keep things professional.

Part of him knew he ought to make an excuse when she offered him coffee. But he was really enjoying her company and it was too hard to resist.

He liked her living room, too. The large window looked out over the salt marshes, and there were watercolours of what he guessed were local scenes on the walls—a stripy lighthouse, bluebell woods, and a sunset over the sea. She had a small TV in one corner, a large bookcase with an eclectic mix of novels and medical textbooks, and a speaker dock for her phone. And there were lots of framed photographs on the mantelpiece· with another woman who looked so much like her that she had to be Toni's sister, with a couple he assumed were her parents, and with an elderly woman he guessed was her grandmother.

Archie trotted into the room behind them; when Toni sat down, the dog sat with his chin on her knee, looking imploringly up at her.

'All right, then.' She lifted her hands and the dog hopped up lightly, settling himself on her lap. She gave Ben a rueful smile. 'He's too big to be a lapdog, really, but he's sat on my lap like this ever since he was tiny.'

Just to prove the point, the dog closed his eyes and started snoring softly.

Ben was shocked by how at home he felt here, how relaxed. His own—rented—accommodation was really just a place to eat and sleep and store his things, and his house in London hadn't been the most relaxing place for the last year he'd lived there. But here… Here, he felt a kind of peace that had escaped him for a long time. And how unexpected that it was in Toni's company—and that of her dog. He wasn't sure whether it reassured him more or scared him. Maybe both.

'I ought to make a move,' he said. 'Can I wash up, first?'

'No, you're fine.'

'Then thank you for dinner.'

'Thank you for pudding,' she said, gently ushering the dog off her lap and standing up.

'See you tomorrow morning.'

'Afternoon,' she reminded him. 'Wednesday mornings during term time is Archie's session at infant school.'

'Enjoy your reading,' he said.

'We will.'

He looked at the dog and took a deep breath. 'Bye, Archie.'

The spaniel, as if realising that Ben couldn't quite cope with making a fuss of him, gave a soft and very gentle 'woof'.

And all the way home Ben couldn't stop thinking about Toni Butler's smile.

He was really going to have to get a grip.

CHAPTER THREE

TONI ALWAYS ENJOYED her reading morning at the school and the enthusiasm of the children; but on Wednesday she couldn't get Ben Mitchell out of her head. She still had no idea why he'd moved from London to their little village on the coast; she had a feeling that it had something to do with the fact that he was single, but she wasn't going to pry.

Because then she would have to admit to the mistake she'd made in dating Sean—a man who only cared about himself and appearances. Sean might be a brilliant surgeon, but he didn't have a scrap of empathy and he was utterly selfish when it came to his personal life. How on earth had she missed that for so long, let herself be blinded to it by his charm?

Well, she knew the answer to that one. Probably because he was so charming. She'd been completely bowled over by him, by the dinners out and weekends away and surprise bouquets of two dozen deep red roses. But it wasn't just being spoiled; she'd done her best to spoil him back, surprise him with good tickets to a show. She'd enjoyed his company. They'd had fun together. And everything had been fine until her grandmother fell ill; then, Toni had found out the hard way that Sean's charm was all surface and he wasn't prepared to support her or put her needs first. She'd been so sure he was The One that his ultimatum had shocked her to the core. She'd fallen out of love with him very quickly after that.

Funny, she'd disliked Ben almost on sight when he'd criticised Archie, assuming that he was another man like Sean—the hot-shot and very self-assured doctor from London who threw his weight around. Yet he'd apologised for being short with her and he'd made an effort with Archie, even though he wasn't a dog person. He'd tried to meet her halfway.

Sean would have expected her to put the dog in the garden as soon as he arrived. Then again, Sean would have objected to a single dog hair sullying the pristine gorgeousness of his overpriced designer suit.

She shook herself. This really wasn't going anywhere. As she'd told her sister, she didn't want a relationship. Didn't *need* a relationship. She liked her life as it was. Ben was her colleague; he might become her friend, but that was all she could offer him. She wasn't risking her heart again.

And focusing on work was the only reason why she'd talked Ben into spending his lunch break with her at the harbour to sit on the wall, eating chips and discussing their plans for the project on patient nutrition, she told herself.

'I hope you can see the irony,' Ben said. 'Two medical professionals discussing nutrition for two particular groups of people—'

'—while stuffing our faces with one of the very things we'll ask them to avoid,' she finished. 'Totally. We're utter hypocrites.' She ate another hot, salty chip with relish.

'But you're right about the chips.' He did the same. 'They're more than worth the long run I'm going to take after work tonight to burn them off.'

His eyes were exactly the same greeny-blue as the sea in the harbour, and they crinkled at the corners. For one moment of insanity, Toni was tempted to lean forward and press a kiss to his mouth.

Then she realised that he was looking at her mouth. He looked up to meet her gaze, and her breath caught. Was he leaning towards her, or was it her imagination? She felt her lips parting involuntarily, and panicked. This wasn't a good idea. Yes, Ben was physically gorgeous and he made her laugh for the right reasons—but they'd be crazy to act on this attraction. She couldn't think about him in romantic terms.

Before they could do anything stupid, she shifted her position on the wall. There was a sudden slash of colour in his face, so she was pretty sure he'd been thinking the same thing. He'd been tempted as much as she was, and had come to the same conclusion: that even if sitting together right now felt like a date, it wasn't. This had to be work and nothing else.

'So did Archie fall asleep this morning when the children read to him?' Ben asked.

She was relieved that he'd let her off the hook and changed the conversation to something safe. 'Yes—and when one of them got a bit stuck and stopped, he opened his eyes. I explained that meant he couldn't wait to hear the next bit, we untangled the difficult word together, and everyone was happy.'

'Sounds good. So do you work part time at the practice?' he asked.

'Given that I'm off on Monday afternoons and Wednesday mornings, you mean? No— we're open from eight until six, and until eight on Thursday evenings. I stay the whole day on Thursday, so that makes up my official thirty-seven and a half hours per week.'

'What about the nutrition project? If we do it as a course, that will take another couple of hours a week.'

She shook her head. 'That's not work. That's giving something back to the community.'

Which was what she did on her Monday afternoons and Wednesday mornings off, too. Toni Butler was definitely one of the good guys. Ben couldn't understand how he'd managed to clash with her at all on Monday.

But this wasn't about his feelings towards Toni. This was work.

Together, they finished the plan to pitch to Ranjit.

And then Ben asked what had been bugging him. 'What's in the bag?'

'Yesterday's fish. A little treat for Archie, who absolutely loves fish,' she said.

'So the entire village is in love with your dog?'

'Pretty much.' She grinned. 'The dad of one of my Wednesday readers owns the fish bar. So every time I come in he gives me a bit of yesterday's fish for the dog. Just as Fluffy—the headmistress's cat—gets a regular delivery.'

Ben had liked the closeness of his community in Chalk Farm, but Great Crowmell was in another league altogether.

'So everyone knows everyone here,' he said.

'And looks out for everyone, too. It's an amazing place to grow up in.' She smiled. 'Sometimes I found it a bit frustrating when I was a teenager—if I was going to a party and I tried to buy a bottle of wine or something, the shop assistants all knew how old I was and refused to sell it to me, and Gran would hear about it on the grapevine before I even got home and then she'd tell me off. But on the flip side it means that when it's icy, none of the elderly people in the village has to go out and risk a fall because someone will go and pick up their shopping or post letters for them; and, if you break your arm, like my neighbour has, there are people who are more than happy to help by driving you wherever you need to go.' She smiled. 'I guess some people would find it a bit stifling, with everyone knowing everyone else's business, but Stacey and I love it here.'

Ben remembered her telling him why she'd moved here at the age of twelve. 'Losing your parents so young must've been really hard.' He couldn't imagine how it would feel to have grown up without his parents.

She nodded. 'But Gran was here, and everyone in the village was really supportive. It's nice that I can still talk about my parents with people who remember them—and about Gran. It means that the three of them are still with me, in a way.'

'What made you go to London for your training?' he asked.

'I was a teenager. Although I love it here, when I was eighteen I kind of wanted the whole bright lights city living thing. And I'm glad I went. It gave me a lot of experience, especially in the emergency department.' She paused. 'What about you? Did you train in London?'

'Yes. I grew up there.'

'You must miss your family.'

'I do. But I wanted to get out of London.' He'd needed a fresh start, away from the people who'd hurt him so badly. Ben hadn't just lost his wife and the baby he'd thought was his, he'd lost the man who'd been his best friend for almost half a lifetime, since they'd met on their first day at university. His best man, who'd been in love with Ben's wife all along.

Why hadn't he seen that?

He'd thought that Patrick didn't like Karen very much but put up with her for his sake. He hadn't had a clue that Patrick had fallen in love with her the very first time he'd met her, and the three years Patrick had spent in Edinburgh immediately after the wedding had been all about putting some space between them. Ben hadn't had a clue that his wife had fallen for Patrick, either. Patrick, the hot-shot surgeon everyone loved working with because he did his best for his patients and for his team. The man who worked one day a week in Harley Street—but always *pro bono*, for children with cleft palates or facial disfigurements. The man who made everyone's life brighter by just being there.

'Ben?' Toni looked concerned.

'Sorry. Wool-gathering.' And nothing was going to drag his thoughts out of him. He'd make something up if she asked him anything more. Instead, he switched the conversation back to their nutrition project.

Later that afternoon, they pitched the idea to Ranjit.

'Brilliant,' the head of the practice said. 'If you do a class, where would you hold it?'

'Hopefully the high school, so we can use their ovens,' Toni said. 'If not, the village hall. Or we can start with a blog or something on the website, and then maybe talk one of the local chefs into doing a demo for us. Actually, that'd be a good fundraiser for the village hall, so I'll bring that one up with the committee.'

'And that would open it up to all our patients,' Ben said. 'People who want to maybe eat more healthily but they've read so much confusing stuff on the internet that they don't know what they should be focusing on.'

'Let me know if you need anything from me,' Ranjit said.

'It's my diabetes clinic tomorrow,' Toni said. 'I can talk to my patients about it and see what they'd like us to do.'

Ben smiled. 'Once you get an idea, you really don't hang about, do you?'

'Life's very short and I'm a great believer in seizing the day. When I'm old, I won't look back and have regrets about all the things I wish I'd done.' She had a few regrets, but she pushed them back where they belonged. You couldn't have everything you wanted, and she was grateful for all the things she did have. Wanting more was just greedy.

Over the next couple of weeks, Ben felt that he had really settled into Great Crowmell. He'd got used to his new routines and his team mates at the practice; and, although he missed the stunning views over London from Primrose Hill on his morning runs, he discovered that he really liked the beach, hearing the swish of the waves against the sand and the cry of the seagulls.

On the Monday evening, he made blondies for the team meeting in the morning. This time, at the meeting, Toni took one of the cakes with her coffee. 'Oh, wow. These are amazing,' she said.

How bad was it that he felt utterly gratified?

Worse still, when she smiled at him, his

heart skipped a beat. Part of him felt as if he was thawing out, coming back to life; but part of him was unsure.

He was really going to have to keep a grip on his emotions. She'd made it clear that she was interested in dating him, but he knew he couldn't trust his judgement. Although he realised Toni wasn't the sort to hurt someone deliberately, neither was Karen and she'd still hurt him.

He was still brooding about it when he saw his last patient of the day, Courtney Reeves. She was seventeen, and was in the middle of doing her A-level exams. He guessed that she wanted to talk to him about anxiety management, because she'd refused to tell the receptionist what was wrong when she'd made an appointment.

'What can I do for you, Courtney?' he asked.

She bit her lip. 'I'm in a mess.'

'OK,' he said. 'Do you feel you can talk to me about it? Or would you prefer someone else to be here with you when we talk? Your mum?'

'I… I can't tell my mum. Please don't tell my mum.' She burst into tears.

Ben handed her the box of tissues on his

desk. 'Anything you tell me is completely confidential. Your medical records are completely private,' he reassured her. 'The only time I will talk to someone else about you is if I think you're in danger, but I'll always talk to you about that first.'

'I've got a place at Cambridge,' she said. 'If I get my grades.'

'And that's where you want to go?' he asked. Or maybe her parents were putting pressure on her to go there and she was finding the extra stress hard to handle.

'I do.' She looked miserable. 'But I've messed it all up.'

He waited until she was ready to start talking. Eventually, she rubbed her eyes. 'I… There was a party. I had too much to drink. I did something really stupid.' She swallowed hard. 'It was a month ago.'

Now he could guess exactly what was wrong. She'd had unprotected sex with someone. 'And now your period is late?' he asked quietly.

She nodded. 'I caught the bus to Norwich and bought a test and did it in the loos at the library—if I'd bought one here someone would've told my mum.'

'And it was positive?' he checked.

She nodded. 'And I don't know what to do. I know I should've got the morning-after pill but I didn't want my mum to know I'd been so stupid and had unprotected sex, and then it was Monday and it was too late.'

'Have you told anyone else?' he asked. 'Is there a counsellor at school you can talk to?'

'Just my best friend. She made me come to see you. She's waiting outside for me.'

'You've got a really good friend there, and you've done exactly the right thing in coming to see me,' Ben said. 'OK. So you've done the test and it's positive. Do you have any other early pregnancy symptoms?'

'Morning sickness, you mean? No. I feel fine. Just that I missed my period. I thought it was because I was stressed over the exams, but I'm always regular. Always.'

He looked at her. 'I'm not judging you, Courtney, but as you didn't use a condom it's possible that you might have picked up an infection, so it might be a good idea to do a swab test.'

'An STD, you mean?' She shook her head. 'It was the first time, for both of us. And I know that for definite.'

'Have you told your boyfriend?'

'And ruin his life as well as mine? How

can I?' she asked. 'He's supposed to be going to Oxford.'

And he didn't want the hassle of a baby? Not that Ben would be mean enough to ask. 'Let's talk about your options,' he said. 'If you want to keep the baby, we can start your antenatal care now.'

'I don't want the baby,' she said. 'I'm too young. I'm just not ready for this.' Her face had lost all its colour. 'But the idea of having a termination… That's…' She grimaced. 'I do Biology A-level, so I know right now it's a tiny bunch of cells, not an actual b…' Her voice tailed off. 'I hate this, Dr Mitchell. I don't know what to do. Whatever I do feels wrong. Someone's going to get hurt. I don't…' She shook her head in anguish, clearly unable to speak because she was fighting back the tears.

'It's a hard decision,' he said. 'And you don't have to make it right away because it's still very early in the pregnancy. You have options. If you don't want to keep the baby but you don't want a termination, you can have the baby adopted and take a gap year between now and university. Or I can refer you to the hospital or clinic for assessment if you feel you'd rather have a termination.

Whatever you decide, Courtney, the main thing is you're not on your own. We can support you here at the practice.'

'My mum's going to be so angry.' Courtney dragged in a breath. 'She had me when she was seventeen and she's always regretted it. I mean, I know she loves me, but if she hadn't had me her life would've been so different. I've heard her talking to people when she thinks I can't hear. If she hadn't had me, she wouldn't be a single mum. She would've gone to university and travelled the world and got an amazing job.' She shook her head. 'And now I've done exactly the same thing she did. She's going to be so disappointed in me.'

'When she's got over the initial shock of the news,' Ben said, 'she might be the best person you can talk to about it. She's been in your shoes, so she knows exactly how it feels.'

'I've let her down,' Courtney said. 'I've let everyone down. And I was supposed to be going to study medicine. How can I possibly be a doctor when I've done something like this?'

'You're human. And plenty of medics I know have had an unplanned pregnancy.' His ex-wife's pregnancy hadn't been planned, either, and he was a medic. Not that it was appropriate to talk about that to Courtney.

'You need to talk things over with your mum,' he said. 'There's no rush. You have plenty of time to make a decision. Think about what you want. And if you'd like me to be there when you tell your mum, or if you'd like someone else you know from the practice to be there, we can arrange that.'

Another tear leaked down her cheek. 'You'd do that?'

'Of course I would. We want to help you, Courtney. You're not alone.'

She looked as if she couldn't quite believe it.

'Find out when's a good time for your mum, and we'll make an appointment to talk to her together,' he said. 'It's all going to work out.'

By the time she left his consulting room, Courtney looked a lot happier. But Ben couldn't stop thinking about Karen. She must've been just as dismayed when she'd realised that she was pregnant. Courtney at least knew who the father was; for Karen, it had been more complicated. Her fling with Patrick had happened while he was away on a course. Given the timing, as soon as she knew she was pregnant she'd realised that there was a strong chance that the baby was Patrick's. She'd panicked, not knowing what to do and not being able to talk to Ben about it because he was part of the problem.

The truth had come tumbling painfully out the day she'd got the appointment for the twenty-week scan.

He blew out a breath. It was pointless making himself miserable about it and wondering where he'd gone wrong. Karen had told him he hadn't done anything wrong. She'd just fallen in love with Patrick. They'd both fought against it, not wanting to hurt him—but then he had been sent away on that course, Patrick had taken Karen to a show in his place, and the emotions had spilled over into kissing and that single night in Patrick's bed.

Although they'd kept apart after that, the guilt and worry had eaten away at Karen, and the upcoming scan had been the last straw. Not wanting to lie to Ben any more, she'd told him the truth. Told him that she wanted Patrick. And, even if the baby turned out to be Ben's, she'd fallen out of love with him and she wanted to make her life with Patrick instead.

Ben had been horrified. What if the baby *was* his? What then?

But Karen had been adamant. Either way, she didn't want to be married to Ben any more. If the baby was his, they'd come to some sort of access arrangement, but she didn't want to live with him for the baby's sake. It wouldn't be fair on any of them.

As for finding out who was the baby's father, she'd done some research on the Internet. She'd found a non-invasive test, based on a simple blood sample from her and a mouth swab sample from himself and Patrick. The sample would analyse the cell-free foetal DNA in her blood—avoiding the risk of miscarriage that could be caused by an invasive test such as chorionic villi sampling—and it would compare genetic markers between the baby's DNA, Patrick's and Ben's. Five thousand of them, so the test would be conclusive.

And so they'd all done the test. Karen had stayed at her mother's for the two weeks it took for the results to come back, not having any contact with either Ben or Patrick until she knew for sure which of them was the father. Ben hadn't wanted to see Patrick, to hear his excuses—plus he didn't trust himself not to be so overwhelmed with emotion that he'd actually punch his ex-best friend.

Those two weeks had been the longest of his life. The seconds had dripped by like treacle. Although they knew that a court of law wouldn't recognise the test, instead asking for a post-natal DNA test for final proof, everything Ben had read about the procedure and the results told him that there was a probability of ninety-nine point nine per cent of inclusion and one hundred per cent of exclusion. That was more than good enough for him.

At least Karen had told him the results face to face. She'd actually given him the results sheet so he could see it for himself.

Patrick was the baby's father.

And Ben's world had imploded.

He'd lost everything. His wife, his baby and his best friend.

He tried to push the thoughts away and finished writing up his notes.

There was a rap at his door.

'Yes?' he called with irritation.

The door opened. 'Ben, I was wondering—' Toni began.

'What now?' he snapped—then hated himself for being so rude. It wasn't her fault and he shouldn't take it out on her. 'Sorry,' he muttered. 'I didn't mean to snap at you.'

'What's wrong?' she asked.

'Nothing.'

'Uh-huh,' she said. And he didn't blame her for not believing him.

'I get that you might not want to talk,' she said, 'but right now you look like crap. Why don't you come running with me? It'll make you feel better.'

Part of Ben wanted to tell her to mind her own business, because he was just fine—except he wasn't fine. And he knew that Toni had a point. The endorphins from going for a run would help his mood, and the sheer mechanics of running, putting one foot in front of the other, would clear his head. Plus it would be nice not to be alone with his thoughts. 'OK,' he said finally.

'Get your running stuff and meet me in the car park outside Scott's Café in half an hour,' she said.

When he drove into the car park, Toni was already there, dressed for a run, leaning against her car with the dog sitting patiently next to her.

Remembering the other night, he put out his hand; the dog took a sniff and then licked his hand. Instead of feeling repulsed, Ben felt warm inside, which he hadn't expected. Comfort from a dog. He would never have guessed that was possible.

'No talking. Just run, when we're on the beach, because I think you need this,' she said, and led the way down the wooden steps to the dog-friendly end of the beach. She let Archie off the lead and began running when the dog raced off.

It had been a long, long time since Ben had run with anyone. And he was truly grateful that Toni didn't push him to talk. The tide was out, and they just ran, both adjusting their stride so they were running side by side. There were other dog-walkers on the beach; Archie bounded up to one or two, whose owners clearly knew Toni and put up a hand in acknowledgement as they passed.

They ran all the way to the dunes, where she stopped. 'Hydration break,' she said. Obviously this was something she did a lot with Archie, because her small backpack held bottles of water and a bowl for the dog. She poured a bowl of water for the dog first, then looked at Ben. 'Did you remember to bring some water?'

'I forgot,' he admitted. His thoughts had been too full of the past.

She handed him a bottle. 'Here you go. It's a new bottle and it's chilled.'

'Thanks.'

She waited until he'd finished drinking before she asked softly, 'Do you want to talk about it?'

Yes and no. Part of him wanted to bury it, but part of him knew it was better to let it out before the memories turned even more poisonous and made him miserable. He blew out a breath. 'This is all in confidence, yes?'

'Of course.'

'One of my patients is pregnant—it wasn't planned and she was pretty upset about it. And I guess it stirred up a few memories for me.'

She waited, not interrupting or asking questions. Just as he did with patients when he wanted to give them the space to talk, knowing that eventually they would fill the silence.

'My wife—ex-wife—was pregnant,' he said quietly. 'Two years ago. The pregnancy wasn't planned.' He had to swallow the lump in his throat. 'And the baby wasn't mine.'

She reached over to squeeze his hand briefly. 'That's a tough situation.'

'It was a mess.' Which was the understatement of the year. It had broken him.

'Had you been married for long?' she asked.

'Five years. I'd just started getting broody. I was thrilled when she told me she was pregnant. I was really looking forward to being a dad. But it all went wrong.' He gave her a wry smile. 'But I guess we both made a mistake. I wasn't the one she really wanted.'

'So how did you find out?'

'She told me, when she got the appointment for the twenty-week scan. She didn't want to lie to me any more. So we did a prenatal paternity test.'

Her eyes widened. 'CVS?'

'No. We didn't want to do anything invasive. It was a blood test for her and mouth swabs with me and...' What would she say if he told her who the other man was? His best friend, the man he'd loved like a brother?

But he didn't want her pity.

He shrugged. 'The other guy. Nothing I could say or do would change what happened. Karen and I had a long talk that night, and she admitted they'd had a fling while I was away and the timing meant she wasn't quite sure who the father was, him or me. What I'd thought was pregnancy hormones making her snappy with me—it wasn't that at all. She felt guilty and angry with herself, and she couldn't help taking it out on me.'

'That's tough for both of you.'

He nodded. 'When I found out, I was so hurt and angry. And the DNA tests showed that the baby wasn't mine. That broke me a bit. But talking to my patient today has made me think about what my ex went through. She was in a mess. The baby was going to change everything. And she did love me when she married me. It was just...' He shrugged. 'She fell out of love with me and in love with him.'

'Did he love her?'

Ben nodded. 'He always had. He tried to fight it for my sake.'

'So you were friends?'

He might as well tell her the whole sorry truth. And if she started pitying him, he'd walk away. 'Yes. He didn't seem to like her very much and he always seemed to avoid her. It never occurred to me that there might be another reason why he did it—like that film my sister, Jessie, watches every single Christmas, where Andrew Lincoln stands in the doorway with those oversized flashcards and tells Keira Knightley that he'll always love her, even though she's married to his best friend.'

He grimaced. 'Jessie always said that was so romantic—but it really isn't. Not when you're on the other end of it and you realise that everyone's lied to you. And *everyone* gets hurt. That's not love.' He looked away. 'After Karen and I got married, Patrick moved to Edinburgh for three years. He told me it was for the sake of his career—but in hindsight I realise that it was actually to put some space between himself and Karen. To keep her out of temptation's reach. But it happened anyway.'

'It sounds like one of those situations where, whatever happened, you were all going to get hurt,' she said gently, taking his hand and squeezing it briefly. 'That's rough.'

He risked a glance at her. There was definitely sympathy in her eyes—but to his relief there was no pity. 'Yeah.'

She waited, giving him a chance to spill the rest.

So he did.

'The baby wasn't mine, so there was no fight over custody. She went to be with him, and we tried to sort everything out without making it any worse than it already was.'

'Did you stay in your house?' she asked.

He nodded. 'Until we managed to sell it. Then I rented somewhere near the surgery where I worked. But I got sick of facing all the pity and then all the matchmakers who were so convinced that if they found Ms Right for me everything would be OK again. That's why I jumped at the idea of coming here. It meant a new start, where nobody knew what had happened.'

'I can understand that,' she said, sounding heartfelt. 'And what you've just told me will stay strictly confidential, I promise you.'

He believed her. 'Thank you.' He gave her a wry smile. 'It's pretty much put me off the idea of marriage and relationships.'

'Hardly surprising. If it makes you feel any better,' she said, 'I'm not very good at picking Mr Right, either.'

'No?' He hadn't expected that. He'd already worked out that Toni was very capable.

'When Gran was first diagnosed with dementia, my ex said that Stacey and I should put her straight in a nursing home. He pretty much gave me an ultimatum—if I came back here to help Stacey look after Gran, we were through, because he didn't want to live in a backwater and he didn't want to have to drive to the middle of nowhere every time he wanted to see me.'

Now he understood those brief shadows in her eyes when she'd talked about London. 'That,' Ben said, 'is incredibly selfish. Especially as I'm guessing he knew that she looked after you when your parents were killed and you grew up here.'

'Exactly. It wasn't a difficult choice.' She smiled grimly. 'I told him that he needn't bother giving me an ultimatum because we were through anyway. And it took him all of half a week to replace me.'

'What an idiot,' Ben said.

She laughed. 'Yes. He was a total stereotype: the epitome of an arrogant surgeon. I should've listened to the theatre nurses who said he was vile to work with.'

'I know the sort.' Patrick was a surgeon, too. But he wasn't arrogant. He was one of the good guys. Which made it hurt even more: how could such a nice guy betray him like that? Ben still didn't understand. 'You're worth more than that.'

'You bet I am. But, actually, I like my life as it is. I love my job, I love being part of this community, and my closest family live nearby. Wanting anything more would be greedy.'

'I should be grateful for what I have, too,' Ben said. Instead of wishing things were different and that he'd been enough for Karen.

'You've got a great job, you're finding your place in a brilliant community, you've got the sea on your doorstep and right now the sun is shining. It doesn't get better than this,' Toni said.

He lifted his empty water bottle in a toast. 'I would drink to that, so just pretend there's some water left.'

She smiled. 'Come back for dinner, if you like, and we can make that toast with wine. It won't be anything fancy, though. Just whatever's in the fridge or I can dig up from the garden.'

'You cooked for me last time, so it's my turn. Plus it will prove I'm capable of making more than just cake.'

'As friends,' she said.

'As friends,' he agreed. Which was the

sensible thing to do. Even though regret twinged through him, because in another time and in another place they might have been more than just friends. Much more.

'Then thank you. That will be lovely. Archie can keep Shona company,' she said. 'And I'll bring pudding. You don't have to worry about allergies or food dislikes—absolutely anything is fine by me. Well, except chocolate cake, but you know about that already.'

'I do indeed. Let's run back to the car.' He paused. 'And thank you for listening, Toni. I think I needed to let that out.'

'Any time,' she said. 'And if you don't want to talk to a human, you can borrow Archie. He won't talk back or ask awkward questions, though he might decide to wash your face.'

And the sweetness in her smile made him want to hug her.

Except they'd just agreed this was a friendship only. He wasn't going to cross the line and spoil it.

CHAPTER FOUR

BACK AT HER HOUSE, Toni showered quickly, popped next door with Archie and made Shona a mug of tea and a sandwich, then collected some strawberries from her garden and a tub of salted caramel ice cream from her freezer before driving over to Ben's house.

Ben had clearly showered and changed into jeans and a T-shirt when he'd got home, and it made him look younger than he did at work—and much more approachable. Though, now he'd told her about his past, she knew she needed to keep her distance. He could offer her friendship and nothing more.

'Hi.' She handed him the strawberries and the ice cream. 'Bit of a cheat, I'm afraid.'

'Are these home-grown strawberries?' he asked.

She smiled. 'Picked just before I walked

out of the door. You can't get much fresher than this or have fewer food miles.'

'And Scott's ice cream. Moira told me on my first day that it was the best ice cream in town; I've tried a few flavours and this one is my favourite. Thank you.'

'Archie loves the doggy ice cream, too,' she said. 'It's really more like frozen yoghurt, so there's no added sugar to wreck his teeth.'

'I'm still getting my head around the concept of ice cream for dogs,' he said. 'Come in. Can I get you a glass of wine?'

'I drove over—so the ice cream didn't melt—so no, thanks—just water for me.' She sniffed appreciatively. 'Something smells nice.'

'The sauce is home-made,' he said, 'but I'm afraid the ravioli and flatbread aren't.'

'I won't hold it against you. I love ravioli and flatbread,' she said.

Ben's house was neat and tidy, but it felt more like a show house than an actual home. There was nothing personal on display; in the kitchen, there were no notes or photographs stuck to the fridge door with a magnet. Her fridge had pictures of family and friends, her shopping list, recipes she wanted to try out from magazines. She hadn't let Sean's behaviour isolate her from the rest of the human race; but, then again, he hadn't betrayed her in the way Ben's wife and his best friend had betrayed him.

If you'd been hurt that much, it was only natural that you'd see your home as a place to sleep, not a place to live. And she'd be very foolish to think she could change the way he felt. He was being polite, but it was obvious to her that he'd shored up all his barriers, not letting anyone close. It felt as if he regretted confiding in her. So it was time to back off, make it clear she was offering him friendship and expecting nothing more. 'Are you busy next weekend?' she asked.

'Yes. I'm keeping up with my professional development,' he said.

Studying? 'In that case, can I tempt you out to play on Saturday?' she asked. 'Just it's the nineteen-forties weekend.'

'Nineteen-forties weekend?'

'You might have seen the posters around the village. Everyone dresses up, all the local businesses join in, and so does the steam train in the next village. And there's a nineteen-forties-themed dance in Great Crowmell Village Hall on the Saturday night. All the proceeds go towards the cost of running events for the local kids over the summer holidays.'

Ben thought about it. Dressing up, a steam train and an evening dancing. It sounded a lot less lonely than the whole weekend spent doing an online course.

'The food is themed as well,' she added. 'So you'll have the delights of corned beef and Spam sandwiches, lentil sausages, homity pie and dairy-free cakes. Oh, and the fish bar is going to have a pop-up stall—on the grounds that fish and chips weren't rationed—and a local brewery is doing the bar. Beer, cider and old-fashioned lemonade.'

'That sounds good. Where do I get a ticket?'

'For the steam train, you buy one at the station. But I can organise your ticket for the dance,' she said with a smile.

'Thanks. Let me know how much I owe you.'

'Will do. And, if you fancy baking some scones to a wartime recipe, the Village Hall committee would love you for ever.'

The penny dropped. 'You're on the committee, aren't you?'

'Yup,' she confirmed. 'We do all sorts of things. There's a dog show later in the summer.'

'Why do I get the feeling that was your idea?' he asked wryly.

She grinned. 'It wasn't, actually, but I'm organising it this year, so Archie isn't allowed to enter any of the classes. He did win the classes for Waggiest Tail and Most Handsome Dog last year, though. If he hadn't, I think there would've been a riot in the infant school and the nursing home. I can just see them now, chanting, "Archie has the waggiest tail!"'

He couldn't help smiling. Toni Butler made him feel light at heart. She really was a ray of sunshine. Why on earth had her ex given her that stupid ultimatum instead of following her here and applying for a surgeon's post at one of the local hospitals? It wouldn't have been that arduous a commute; in fact, it would probably have been a shorter journey to work than he'd had in London.

But that was straying into dangerous territory.

Yes, he'd confided in Toni, but he didn't

want to risk getting closer, even though at the same time he yearned for that closeness. Despite his reservations, he found himself asking her to stay just a bit longer— for two cups of coffee after dinner—and he refused to let her even look at the washing up.

'I'd better get back,' she said at last. 'I need to pick up Archie from Shona, and I promised to wash her hair for her this evening. Until it happens to you, I don't think you realise how much you can't do when you break your arm; even though it's not her writing hand, there are so many things she finds tricky. And being in plaster during the summer...' She wrinkled her nose. 'Really not fun.'

'Poor woman. Let me know if I can do anything to help,' he said.

'Bake me that dozen scones,' she said. 'I'll email you the wartime recipe.'

'Great. Enjoy your reading morning with Archie at the school tomorrow.' He saw her to the door. 'And thank you for today. For listening and not...' He shrugged awkwardly. 'Not judging.'

'Any time,' she said. 'That's what friends are for.'

It suddenly struck him that she was right:

they had become friends over the last couple of weeks. And it warmed him all the way through. Even though a little voice in his head was whispering that he'd like her to be more than his friend...

The following week, on the Saturday morning, Ben made scones to the wartime recipe that Toni had sent over—which, to his surprise, included grated carrot. He made two dozen, and they'd cooled by the time Toni came to pick him up.

'*Two* dozen? Thank you, you superstar,' she said with a smile. Then she looked him up and down. 'And you look pretty much perfect, as a nineteen-forties village doctor—pleated trousers, checked shirt, Fair Isle sleeveless jersey, fedora and a tweed jacket.'

'Thank you. I hired my costume, though obviously the stethoscope is modern.'

'You hired your costume from Moira's cousin?' she guessed.

'Yes. You look very nice, too.' She was wearing a pale blue cotton tea dress decorated with bright red peonies, cream sandals with a strap around the ankle and a low kitten heel, and her hair was put up in a neat roll. Her lipstick matched the peonies on her dress, and Ben really had to fight the urge to kiss her.

'Thank you. Stacey made the dress for me.'

'Is she coming today?'

'Definitely. You'll get to meet her later. Shall we go?' she asked. 'We just need to drop these off at the village hall, and then we can head down the coast to catch the train.'

They dropped off his scones and her mini homity pies, then parked on the outskirts of the next town round the coast and walked to the train station.

The streets were absolutely crammed with people, and the only cars that were parked in the High Street were vintage ones. A couple of policemen arrested a spiv who was offering people watches from the inside of his jacket; servicemen in uniform walked alongside Land Girls carrying baskets of eggs and old-fashioned milk cans; and several children were dressed as evacuees, carrying a teddy and a gas mask box and with labels tied around their necks. The shops and cafés had all joined in, with sandbags piled outside the doors and brown tape stuck to the windows in cross formation; even the window displays were vintage, from sweets to clothing to groceries. There was bunting everywhere, pop-up stalls offered to do vintage make-up and hair, and in a corner of the village square a stage was set up for singers to perform using an old-fashioned microphone.

'This is amazing,' he said. 'How long has this event been going?'

'A couple of decades, now. It started with a few steam railway enthusiasts setting up a weekend, not long after Stacey and I moved in with Gran, and it just snowballed, with more people joining in every year. Gran used to love this. And we loved going with her, because she used to tell us all her childhood memories and about what life was like growing up in wartime, and we'd look through all the old photo albums—from Mum's childhood as well as Dad's.' She took his hand. 'Come on. Let's go and get our tickets for the steam train.'

There were soldiers and sailors everywhere, women sporting fox fur tippets that Ben rather hoped were fake, others wearing overalls with scarves tied round their heads, and men dressed as the Home Guard. The train was crammed with people, and the carriages were vintage with a corridor for the guard and two bench seats per compartment that stretched across the whole width of the compartment and a metal and rope netting shelf above the seats for luggage.

'Room for two,' the guard said, and made everyone squash up. He grinned at them. 'We can seat six a side. And remember there's a war on.'

Toni insisted that Ben have the window seat, and he was stunned by the glorious view of the sea across the cornfields.

'This is quite an experience. I can't ever remember travelling on a steam train before,' he said. 'I loved all the stories about trains when I was small, but we never went anywhere like this as a family.'

'My mum and dad loved it. Steam trains had been phased out in favour of diesel by the time my parents were born, but Gran remembered being on a steam train when she was younger and she and my grandad used to take us on this one when we were small,' Toni said.

'When I was a kid and my favourite books talked about the trains making a "chuff-chuff" sound, I thought it was just the story, but they really do make that sound. It's amazing,' he said.

'And look, you can see the steam coming past the window,' she said.

There was a faint smell of sulphur in the air, which Ben assumed was from the coal. And it really did feel as if he'd gone back in time.

At the end of the line, there was a small funfair with old-fashioned steam gallopers and swing-boats, and stalls with old-fashioned games.

'Going to win me a coconut, Dr Mitchell?' she teased.

When he won her a coconut first time and presented it to her with a bow, she laughed. 'You've done this before, haven't you?'

'No. But I played cricket a lot when I was younger.'

'Remind me to introduce you to Mike, who runs the village cricket team,' she said.

The tea tent had notices everywhere telling people not to waste sugar as it was on ration, and there were old-fashioned cakes on sale.

'This is great,' Ben said. 'I haven't had this much fun in...' he paused '... I don't know when.'

'Good.' She smiled at him, and again his heart skipped a beat.

Back in Great Crowmell, once they'd dropped her car at her house and were walking towards the harbour, she grew more serious. 'Are you sure you're all right about meeting Stacey, Nick and Scarlett? I mean— I understand if it'll be too…' She paused, as if trying to find the right word.

Ben knew what she meant. He'd thought he'd be a dad, and then it had been taken away from him. Being around a small child would remind him of what he didn't have.

'It's fine,' he reassured her, though he appreciated the fact that she'd thought about what he'd told her. 'Remember, I treat babies and small children at the surgery—and parents who bring their babies with them.'

'Just as long as I'm not ripping the top off the scab.'

'It's fine,' he said.

And when he met Stacey, he liked her immediately; she was as warm and kind as Toni. Their grandmother must've been a really special woman, he thought.

'Ice creams are on me,' Nick said, leading them towards Scott's.

'I keem!' Scarlett crowed happily from her very old-fashioned pram.

'It's borrowed,' Stacey told him, having clearly noticed his glance at the pram. 'It's amazing what's survived from seventy years ago. This is the kind of thing our great-grandmother would have used—though I have to say it's way heavier than Scarlett's pram and it doesn't fold up, so it'd be a nightmare to try and put this in a car.'

'I've never been to this sort of fundraising thing before,' Ben said. 'And to think that the whole village is involved—well, several villages—is incredible.'

'It's a good community, here,' Stacey told him.

Which he was really beginning to feel part of, thanks to Toni. And here, where nobody except Toni knew his past, he was finally healing. The bleak emptiness that had stretched out in front of him in London didn't feel quite so bleak any more. He met Toni's neighbour Shona properly, too, and Toni made a point of introducing him to the cricket club captain, Mike.

Weirdly, Ben felt more at home here than he ever had at Chalk Farm. How was that even possible?

At seven, they headed for the village hall, which had been thoroughly decorated with bunting, sandbags and tape on the windows. Inside, there were trestle tables for the food, covered in white tablecloths, and with vintage china cake stands and dishes for the food.

'So the community has all come together for this?' Ben asked. 'All the food is donated?'

'We all either grew up here and benefited from the generosity of people in the past, or we've got kids who use it now. The village hall organises stuff for all age groups and as I mentioned, the money raised means we can run events for the kids free during the summer holidays, and keep everything else down to a reasonable cost,' Toni explained. 'So whether it's the toddler group, the senior citizens' afternoon tea dances, or youth club evenings, which can be anything from a talent competition through to self-defence classes and archery lessons, there's something for everyone.' She looked at him. 'Surely you had stuff like this in London?'

'Not really,' he said.

'Well, there you go—another benefit of living here,' she said.

Just about everyone in the room wanted to talk to Toni, he discovered. And she made sure she introduced him to everyone in the village he hadn't met yet, finding common interests so they had something to talk about, and he wasn't left standing around on his own, feeling awkward.

When the music started, Ben said, 'May I have this dance, Miss Butler?'

'Sure,' she said. 'Though I should warn you that I have two left feet and your toes might regret you asking me.'

'Or maybe they won't. Follow my lead,' Ben said with a smile.

It was nice that Ben had joined in, Toni thought. He'd made scones, he'd hired a costume, and now he was going to dance with her—so very unlike Sean's reaction to the nineteen-forties weekend. When Toni had suggested that he join her family at the event, he'd balked at the idea of wearing anything other than designer jeans and a high-end brand shirt, let alone something vintage. In the end, he hadn't been able to join them because he'd been called to the hospital to treat a complication in one of his patients; but Toni suspected that he'd got someone to make that call rather than say straight out that he didn't want to go.

She expected Ben to be a slightly better dancer than her, but she wasn't prepared for him to be absolutely brilliant, spinning around and leading her on the floor in a way that made her feel as if she could actually dance instead of being her usual hopeless self.

'You're amazing!' she said when she caught her breath. 'You're a dark horse, Ben Mitchell. Where did you learn to dance like *that*?'

'Let's say I had a misspent youth,' he told her with a grin.

And, now he was relaxed and laughing, he was utterly gorgeous, Toni thought. No wonder he was attracting admiring glances from every woman in the room. He was definitely making her own heart go pitapat. Which was crazy, because she knew he didn't want to get involved with anyone. But, just for tonight, maybe she could dream.

'You had dance lessons?'

'Jessie did,' he said.

His sister, she remembered.

'She needed a partner, so I was the obvious choice.'

Because he was her big brother, looking out for her? That didn't surprise Toni. Ben

Mitchell was the sort of man who would've asked his little sister's shy and geeky best friend to the prom so she wasn't left feeling awkward and alone. Kind. Thoughtful. A huge contrast to Sean—how could she ever have thought Ben reminded her of her ex? It might have seemed that way at first but, the more she got to know him, the more she liked him. 'So she learned to do the jive and stuff like that?'

'All the ballroom dances and all the Latin ones,' he said. 'Jessie took all her exams and got gold medals.'

'And so did you?' she guessed.

'To support her,' he said, glossing over the question.

So clearly he'd done well but wasn't the sort to boast about it.

'Our teacher really liked big band music and nineteen-forties dances,' Ben said, 'so she taught us the jitterbug and the Lindy Hop as well.'

'The jitterbug? Now that's *way* above my pay grade,' Toni said, laughing.

'You might be surprised. Let's give it a go.'

He talked her through some of the steps— and, the next thing she knew, she was actually dancing the jitterbug with him, twirling round and actually going in the direction she was supposed to go instead of the complete opposite. And it made her feel as if she was flying.

Though, if she was honest with herself, it wasn't just the dance moves that made her feel so good. It was Ben himself.

Which was dangerous. She knew she wasn't good at relationships, and he was understandably wary. She needed to be sensible.

'I loved that,' she said when the song was over. 'I've never been able to dance anywhere near as well as that before.'

'Who are you and what have you done with my little sister?' Stacey teased, coming over to them with her arm wrapped round her husband. 'Toni, I've never seen you that co-ordinated before. That was amazing.'

'I'm not taking any credit for that. It was all him,' Toni said, gesturing gracefully towards Ben.

'You could be a professional dancer, Ben,' Stacey said.

Ben laughed. 'I'm happy with my current job, but thank you for the compliment.'

'Very much deserved. Dr Mitchell, please may I have the next dance?' Stacey asked.

'Sure.' He held his hand out to her. 'Are you two joining us?'

Nick looked at Toni and shook his head. 'I can't do what you do, Ben—and I value my toes! You and I are going to queue up at the bar and sort out a round, Toni.'

'Perfect,' Toni said, tucking her arm through Nick's.

'Can we get you a beer, Ben?' Nick asked.

'That'd be great, thanks. I'm not fussy what you get,' Ben said. 'And the next round is mine.'

'I like him. He's a nice guy,' Nick said when they were in the queue.

'Don't you start,' Toni warned. 'Or did Stacey prime you to say that?'

'Hey. You're my baby sister-in-law. I worry about you nearly as much as Stacey does,' Nick said.

'I love you, too, big brother-in-law,' Toni said with a smile. 'But I'm fine as I am. Really. You don't have to worry about me.'

In between the odd sip of beer, Ben danced with quite a few of women in the hall— including a virtuoso display with one of the local dance teachers, which had everyone standing around them in a circle, clapping and cheering as they executed amazing spins and turns.

'That man,' Stacey said to Toni, 'is something else.'

Toni knew that tone well. 'He's my colleague,' she reminded her sister.

'And I've seen the way he looks at you. He likes you.'

'Strictly as a friend,' Toni said firmly. And she wasn't going to admit to that wobble in her stomach when he caught her eyes across the dance floor and smiled at her.

'Give him a chance, Toni.'

Toni hugged her. 'I love you, and we've had this conversation a lot of times. We're going to agree to disagree, OK? I'm not good at choosing men, and Ben has his own reasons not to want to get involved. We're friends. End of.'

She signalled to Ben at the end of the dance. 'Want to come and get some food?'

Between them, they got a selection of sandwiches, scones and a couple of the mini homity pies Toni had made earlier.

'So what exactly is a homity pie? A kind of quiche?' Ben asked, looking at the open-topped pies.

'Sort of. Eggs and onions were scarce in the war, so the filling's mainly potato and leek with a chopped apple, one egg and a little bit of cheese,' she said.

'Making do. Yeah. It took me a while to get my head round the idea of putting grated carrots in scones,' Ben said.

'Sugar replacement plus added moisture. Which I guess we still do today; think of carrot cake,' she said.

'So where did you get the recipes?'

'One of the village hall committee has an original wartime recipe book that belonged to her grandmother, so we use that.' She took a bite of one of his scones. 'These are wonderful. If you were in the market for a relationship, between your dancing and your cooking I think you'd have a queue of women a mile long wanting to date you.'

Ben looked at her. He wasn't in the market for a relationship. But if he was, he didn't want a queue of women a mile long. He wanted just one woman.

Toni Butler.

But she'd made it clear she wasn't looking for a relationship and they were just friends.

He wished she hadn't put the idea of relationships into his head when the music turned slower and he ended up dancing with her again; this time, they were cheek to cheek and he could smell the fresh floral scent of her shampoo and feel the warmth of her body in his arms.

He tried mentally naming all the muscles of the body in order from the *triceps surae* to the *occipitofrontalis*, but it didn't switch his attention away from her. So in the end he gave in to the demands of the music and his heart and just held her, swaying with her.

When he pulled back slightly, her pupils were huge and her mouth was slightly parted. All he would have to do was tilt his head slightly and his lips would touch hers. His mouth tingled and his heartbeat was skittering around.

Could he?

Should he?

Was it his imagination, or was she staring at his mouth, too? Did she want him to kiss her? Like that day when they'd sat on the harbour wall, eating fish and chips, and he'd nearly kissed her.

The temptation was too great, and he was about to lean forward and kiss her, just once, when the song ended and the band struck up another fast dance.

'I think your fan club awaits,' she said with a smile.

What could he do but dance the Lindy Hop with the next woman who asked him?

And his dance with Toni turned out to be the last slow dance of the night, so he had no more excuses to pull her back into his arms.

'Can I walk you home?' he asked, really hoping that he wasn't blushing and sounding as bashful as a teenager. 'I mean, I know you're perfectly capable of seeing yourself home, but...'

'That'd be nice,' she said. 'Thank you.'

And somehow on the way home his fingers brushed against hers. Once. Twice. The third time, he let his fingers cling to hers. And by the end of the road they were holding hands. They weren't discussing it or even acknowledging it, but they were definitely holding hands.

At her garden gate, she said, 'Will you come in for a coffee?'

He could be sensible and make an excuse.

Or he could follow the urging of his heart. To look forward instead of back. To consider the enticing possibility of a future.

'Thank you. I'd like that,' he said.

Archie was thrilled to see them and leaped round the kitchen.

'Sit,' Ben said.

To his surprise, Archie actually did what Ben asked.

He held out his hand, let the dog sniff him, then rubbed the top of the dog's head. Archie rewarded him with the gentlest of licks.

'He likes you,' Toni said, and the approval in her voice warmed him all the way through.

'He's a nice dog. And he's gone a long way to—well, making me a bit nicer.'

She smiled and let the dog out into the garden. 'It wasn't that you were totally horrible; we just had a few crossed wires and we got off to a bad start.'

'Thank you.' He smiled back at her. 'Did you enjoy the dance?'

'I always do—but you made it special for me, this year. I've never danced like that before.'

'Seriously? It isn't just family teasing that you can't dance?'

'No. If you ever go to a dance aerobics class with me, I'm the one who's doing all the right moves—but in the wrong direction,' she said with a grin. 'I'm infamous for it. And the men in Great Crowmell only dance with me if they're wearing steel toecaps.'

'You were doing just fine with me.'

She looked at him, her gorgeous grey eyes darkening. 'Can we do that again?'

'The jitterbug?'

'The other one.'

The slow dance. The one that had made his heart beat in a crazy rhythm. 'Sure,' he said. 'We need some music. Let me find some on my phone.'

The next thing he knew, their coffees were ignored and she was in his arms, swaying with him to the soft, slow song.

And this time, when he pulled back and saw the glitter in her eyes, he gave in to the temptation that had been tugging at him all evening and let his mouth brush against hers. Once, very lightly, skimming across her skin.

He felt as if he were going up in flames.

And then her arms tightened around him and she let him deepen the kiss.

He had no idea how long they stayed locked together in the middle of her kitchen, just kissing.

But then reality seeped in.

He hadn't been enough for Karen.

There was no reason why he would be enough for Toni, either.

What was he doing? If this carried on, they were both going to get hurt. Much as he wanted to scoop her up and carry her to her bed, it would be a really reckless, stupid thing to do.

This was meant to be his new start, and he was in severe danger of messing everything up.

They needed to stop this.

Now.

He pulled away. 'Toni. We shouldn't…' He dragged in a breath. 'I need to go.'

Reality crashed in as if Ben had just thrown a bucket of icy water over her.

What had she been doing, letting herself get carried away like that? She knew he didn't want a relationship. He was still licking his wounds after what had happened in London—when his wife had had an affair with someone who was supposed to be his friend, and the result had been a baby that wasn't his.

Maybe in another time, another place, it could have worked out between them. She liked him and, from the way his sea-green eyes had turned almost black, his pupils enormous, she could tell that he liked her.

But this was the wrong time for him; and she'd had enough of making mistakes and falling for Mr Wrong.

Better to keep things strictly platonic.

'Sure,' she said brightly, and squashed the urge to suggest that instead they could act on the pull between them, get it out of their systems and then go back to being strictly colleagues. That was way too reckless and it was so obvious that they would both end up hurt. She was rubbish at relationships. They needed to keep things simple. 'See you at work,' she said.

Once he'd gone, she curled up with her dog.

They'd done the sensible thing, Toni knew. The right thing.

So why did she feel so miserable about it?

'This is ridiculous, Archie,' she told the dog. 'I'm rubbish at relationships. I didn't see past Sean's Mr Charming act—even though I knew Gran and Stacey didn't think that much of him, I made excuses for him and didn't let myself see how selfish he was. The two before him were nearly as bad. And the three guys I've dated since I moved back were all nice men, but there just wasn't a spark between us.' She sighed. 'Am I just an idiot who only falls for awful men?'

Ben Mitchell wasn't an awful man. Far from it. He wasn't selfish. But she was definitely attracted to him every bit as much as she'd been attracted to her last Mr Wrong.

Though Ben was complicated. Vulnerable. He'd been badly hurt and he'd made it clear that, although the attraction was mutual, he didn't want to get involved with anyone.

'Gran would say it would all come out in the wash,' she said. 'Tomorrow we're going for a run at the beach and everything will be fine.'

But even saying it out loud wasn't quite enough to convince herself. She had a feeling it would be really awkward, the next time she saw Ben. How were they going to fix this?

CHAPTER FIVE

TONI SLEPT BADLY that night, full of guilt and longing, and cross with herself for being wet.

'Common sense and sea air to blow the cobwebs out. That's what we need,' she said to the dog.

And then she would throw herself into the rest of the nineteen-forties weekend, meeting up with her sister again and enjoying spending time with people she loved most. She was so, so lucky. She had nothing to whine about and she needed to stop being so self-indulgent and longing for what she couldn't have.

She walked the dog down to the harbour and up to the beach, then went for a run along the shoreline. The sound of the sea and the fresh air did their usual trick of rebalancing her.

'Sausage?' she asked Archie as they reached Scott's Café.

The dog woofed softly in agreement.

She hadn't bothered grabbing more than a banana before they went out, and the café was dog-friendly, so she went in to order a latte, a bacon sandwich and one of the sausages the café kept especially for dogs.

And of course Ben *would* be sitting there in the corner.

So had he, like her, felt antsy enough to need a run to clear his head? Was he as confused as she was?

What should she do now? Give him space, smile and sit in the opposite corner of the café? Or go along with the whole friends and colleagues thing, treat him just as if he were one of the other medics at the practice, sit with him and pretend that kiss had never happened?

She wasn't the dithery sort. What on earth was wrong with her?

He looked wary and confused, too.

That settled it. She'd be professional—and she had Archie as a buffer.

'Hi. Have you been out for a run?' she asked brightly.

'It's the perfect start to a Sunday morning,' he said. And either he was better at pretending than she was, or that kiss had affected him a lot less. 'Obviously you've been for a run, too.'

'Yes. We've just ordered breakfast,' she said.

'Me, too. If Archie is allowed to sit in the café, you're both welcome to join me.'

So they really were going to manage to pretend that kiss last night hadn't happened? They could keep their good working relationship and she hadn't messed it up? That was a relief; and at the same time there was a sneaking sensation of disappointment, too, because it meant that kiss would stay a one-off. And that kiss had awoken all sorts of feelings she'd thought she'd buried. Desire. Need. A coil of lust snaked through her.

She reined in her wayward longings. 'Thanks. That would be good.' She looked at Archie. 'No scrounging, Arch. You've got your own order.'

'I noticed they had sausages for dogs on the menu,' Ben said with a smile. 'I'm assuming it's a regular order for Archie?'

'It is,' she admitted.

Ben's bacon sandwich arrived first.

'Don't let it get cold by waiting for us,' she said, gesturing to him to eat.

'Or we could go halves until yours arrives?' he suggested.

'No, it's fine.' She smiled at him. 'Enjoy.'

He was halfway through the sandwich when he said to her, 'My knee feels warm.'

She groaned, knowing exactly what her dog was doing. 'Give it two minutes and your knee will be wet as well. Sorry.'

'Can I give him a little bit of my sandwich?'

For someone who was a self-confessed non-dog person, Ben had really thawed out towards Archie. 'Sure. But make him sit nicely for it, and he only gets the very last bit when you're done.'

He smiled. 'Got it.'

She could feel the dog inching forward towards Ben under the table. 'Sorry,' she said again.

'It's fine,' he said with a grin and when Archie sat nicely and took the corner of the sandwich very gently from Ben's hand, 'Your dog,' Ben said, 'is definitely winning me over.'

Was there something more in Ben's expression, or was she seeing what she wanted to see?

'That's good,' she said carefully, playing it safe.

They made small talk until her sandwich arrived, and she sliced Archie's sausage for him. Then she looked at Ben and couldn't help smiling. 'Right now you've got the same expression on your face as one of my Wednesday readers.'

Rather than being offended, he laughed. 'Yeah. I guess I know how they feel. Being dog monitor for the day.'

'Feed him the sausage. It's very gratifying. You can get him to do tricks for a piece of sausage—sit, lie down, offer you a paw.' She paused. 'Dare you.'

He tried it.

And Toni thoroughly enjoyed watching the surprise on Ben's face, followed by pleasure as the dog obeyed every single command.

'You're right. It's very gratifying. Like feeding a baby.'

Instantly the shadows were back in his eyes. And she knew why. The baby that wasn't his.

He would've made such a great dad.

And it was hard to come back from a situation like that, to learn to trust again. No wonder he'd moved away from London; a fresh start in a place that held no memories would help him get over it.

But was she the one who could mend his broken heart?

She only seemed to pick the kind of men who were so selfish that she ended up walking away. Sometimes she wondered whether it was because, deep down, she was scared of losing her heart to someone and then losing them the same way she'd lost her parents and her grandmother; by constantly picking Mr Wrong, it meant that she was the one to leave instead of the one who was left behind, sad and lonely. But, if she was honest with herself, she was still lonely anyway.

And Ben was nothing like her exes. That made him more dangerous. If she trusted him with her own heart, would he keep it safe? Or would he be the one to end up walking away, leaving her desolate?

'I'd better let you get on,' he said when she'd finished her sandwich. 'I have an online course sending me nagging emails. See you tomorrow.'

Even though part of Toni wanted to give

him a hug and tell him that not all women were like his ex and he would find someone to love him as he deserved, she didn't. This was a public place and Ben was quite a private man; although he'd been open in the practice meeting about why he was wary of dogs, he hadn't told anyone except Toni about his ex or the baby, and she had no intention of betraying his confidence. 'See you tomorrow,' she said.

But as they walked out of the café they could see a small boy standing on the patio, crying and guarding his arm, with an elderly couple who were presumably his grandparents looking very anxious and clearly trying to persuade him to let them look at his arm.

'That's Jake Flowers,' Toni told Ben, recognising the little boy. 'He's not one of my Wednesday readers, but I went to school with his mum and he's in the same class as some of my readers. Hi there,' she said brightly, going over to them. 'Jake, did you hurt your arm?'

He nodded. 'I fell over. It really hurts.'

'He won't let us touch it,' the elderly woman said.

'I'm a nurse and Ben is a doctor,' Toni reassured her. 'Maybe he'll let us help.' She turned to the little boy. 'You know Archie from school, don't you? He helps some of your friends with reading.'

Jake nodded.

'He thinks Dr Ben and I can help your arm feel better. Will you let us look at it, to stop Archie worrying about you?'

Jake nodded, still a little reluctantly, but stopped guarding his arm.

Ben gently examined him. 'I think when you fell over you dislocated your elbow, Jake. The bones slipped out of place, and that's why it hurts. I can pop it back in for you, so it will stop hurting.'

Though the procedure of fixing the dislocation would really hurt for a brief moment, Toni knew. She needed to do something to distract the little boy so he didn't tense up in anticipation of it hurting and make things worse.

'Tell you what,' she said to Jake. 'To stop Archie worrying, while Dr Ben puts your elbow back in place, can you tell him a joke?'

'I don't know any jokes,' Jake said. His lower lip wobbled.

'What's that, Archie? You know one?' She pretended that the dog was whispering in her ear. 'That's a good one! Jake, what do sea monsters eat?'

'I don't know.'

Toni smiled. 'Fish and ships!'

The little boy smiled, despite himself.

'Oh—he wants your grandad to help him tell the next one.'

The old man looked taken aback, but to her relief he went with it and crouched down next to the dog, pretending that the dog was whispering in his ear, too. 'That's a good one, Archie! What did the sea say to the sand?' he asked.

Jake shook his head.

'Nothing—it just waved!' Jake's grandfather said.

Ben made one swift movement, and Jake cried out—and then he looked surprised. 'Oh! It's stopped hurting. Thank you, Dr Ben.'

'My pleasure. And you were *really* brave. Archie's going to bring you a special sticker from me on Wednesday,' Ben said, 'when he comes to help with reading at your school.'

Jake beamed. 'Really?'

'Really,' Ben promised.

'Thank you so much,' Jake's grandmother said. 'We came down for the nineteen-forties weekend and we thought we would take Jake to the sea and give Lee and Sally a few minutes to themselves, this morning. I feel so bad he fell over and hurt himself.'

'These things happen,' Ben reassured her. 'If his mum and dad had been with you when he fell over, it would probably still have happened.' He examined Jake's arm. 'It looks fine to me. Jake could do with a bit of infant paracetamol because his elbow will still be a little bit swollen and sore for a while, but his arm should be fine. If he's not using his arm as normal by lunchtime, it's worth popping in to the hospital for an X-ray, but I think you'll be just fine.'

'Thank you so much,' Jake's grandfather said. 'I don't know what we would've done if you hadn't been here.'

'I'm glad we could help,' Ben said. 'And don't worry about it happening again. It's probably a one-off. He just needs to be a little bit careful for the next week or so. Archie has got one more joke for you, Jake,' Ben added, and pretended to listen to the dog. 'How do you make an octopus laugh?'

'I don't know,' Jake said.

'With ten tickles!'

The little boy giggled; Ben smiled and stood up.

He was fabulous with children, Toni thought. He would've been an amazing dad. She hoped for his ex's sake that the man she chose, the baby's biological father, would be as good a dad as Ben would've been.

'Enjoy the rest of the nineteen-forties weekend,' Ben said to Jake's grandparents. He smiled at Toni, and headed for his car. Toni said her goodbyes to Jake and his grandparents, and then walked back home with Archie before changing back into her nineteen-forties costume and going over to her sister's.

'Ben not with you today?' Stacey asked.

'He's studying,' Toni said.

'OK.' Stacey looked at her. 'I liked him very much.'

'You've already told me that, Stace,' Toni said with a smile. 'Remember, he's my colleague.'

'You weren't looking at each other like colleagues yesterday,' Stacey pointed out.

No. But she'd got that very badly wrong, hadn't she? 'It was probably just the shock of me managing to dance without bruising someone's toes,' Toni retorted. 'Let's go and see the sights.'

To her relief, Stacey didn't quiz her any further about Ben. And it *was* fine: they were colleagues, and that was that.

CHAPTER SIX

BEN LOOKED AT the screen and sighed. Normally he loved doing professional development, keeping his knowledge up to date and learning about new things that would help his patients. Just today he could hardly concentrate.

And he knew why.

Toni Butler.

Toni, with her lovely grey eyes, her sweet, sweet smile and her amazing warmth.

If he was honest with himself, he'd gone for that run on the beach because he knew that she often went there and he'd been hoping to bump into her 'accidentally'. And then she'd walked into the café.

It would've been so easy to suggest spending the rest of the day together and catching up with his studies that evening. He even liked her dog, which had been a huge surprise to him.

But his head was all over the place. He wasn't in love with Karen any more, but he was still healing from what had happened. When he'd said to Toni that rewarding her dog with slices of sausage for performing tricks was as gratifying as feeding a newborn, it had brought all the regrets flooding back.

He ought to move on.

He wanted to move on.

But Toni had been hurt, too. By a man who sounded as if he'd been full of charm on the surface but deep down was utterly selfish. Ben knew that he wasn't like that, that he would treat her the way she deserved to be treated. But the nagging doubts were in his head. Could he trust again? He didn't think that Toni was the cheating type; then again, he hadn't thought that Karen would cheat on him, either.

Guilt was nagging at him, too. He'd pretty much put a wall of misery between himself and his family, and he'd moved here and let that wall harden. Seeing how close Toni was to her sister made him realise how much he missed his own sister. He'd always enjoyed spending time with her, and it wasn't fair to push Jessie away.

On impulse, he picked up the phone.

Jessie answered within three rings. 'Ben! How are you?'

'Fine. You?'

'Fine, but I miss you. Have you settled in, yet?'

'Yes, I think so.'

'So can we come and see you?'

He loved his family, but his parents had never been particularly good at emotional stuff and he knew he'd end up squirming and wishing he hadn't invited them. 'My place is quite small. Maybe just you, Kit, Kelly and the baby?' His nephew, and Ben was guiltily aware that he hadn't been supportive enough to his sister, because seeing the baby brought back all the might-have-beens.

'Great. It'd be lovely to have a weekend by the sea. How about next weekend?'

'Sorry, I'm rostered on for a shift at the surgery on Saturday.'

'The weekend after?'

'I'm studying.'

'*Ben.*' Her voice was full of disappointment. He'd dangled a promise and then cut it off.

He didn't really have a valid excuse to put her off any longer. And, actually, it would be good to see his sister. 'The week after that?'

'Put it in your diary now. I can't wait. I've missed you,' she said again.

'I've missed you, too,' he admitted. 'There's a nineteen-forties fundraising event here at the moment. There was a dance in the village hall last night—the jitterbug, the Lindy Hop, the lot.'

'Oh, Ben. I wish you'd said. I would've loved to go to that.' She paused. 'Did you dance?'

'Yes. And I dressed up.'

'Good.' She sighed. 'Oh, Ben. I've really missed you.'

'I've missed you, too,' he said softly. 'But I needed to get out of London.'

'After what Karen and Patrick did, you needed a fresh start, I know. And I understand. I just wish you were nearer,' she said 'So have you settled in OK? It's been so hard to get hold of you.'

'Sorry. I've just been a bit busy,' he said. 'I'm doing fine. Really. My new team is great. And our nurse practitioner has a therapy dog. He's a sweetheart and he was very handy today as a distraction when I needed

to put a small child's dislocated elbow back in the right place.'

'GPs don't work on Sundays, and you're not a dog person,' she said. 'So what were you…? Oh! Are you dating the nurse practitioner? What's her name?'

'No. We're colleagues, and we just happened to be at the beach café at the same time. I'm very far from being ready to date anyone, and we're not right for each other anyway. There's no chemistry between us.' It wasn't strictly true, but he needed to head Jessie off before she got too hopeful that he'd finally moved on. He was definitely getting there, and he was beginning to think that maybe Toni was the one who'd help him trust again, but it was still early days. 'I'd better let you get on. See you a week on Friday—and I'll speak to you before then.'

'All right. And I'm glad you called, Ben.'

'Me, too.'

'Love you,' she said softly.

'Love you, too.'

On Monday, Ben went to the surgery armed with dog treats.

'Who are you and what have you done

with the scary doctor who disapproves of my dog?' Toni teased.

'A reformed man who has been through impromptu aversion therapy,' Ben retorted. 'And less of your cheek, Nurse Practitioner Butler, unless you want me to organise a dancing demonstration at the village hall with you as the star turn.'

'Bring it on,' she said. 'I don't mind making a fool of myself, if it raises funds. But your toes might want a word with your mouth later for suggesting it.'

Ben couldn't help grinning. He really liked this woman. If only he could be enough for her. But he couldn't quite let himself believe that he'd be enough for anyone. 'You keep her in check, Archie,' he said, and ruffled the fur on the top of the dog's head.

Every single one of his female patients that morning commented either on his dancing or his scones, and half the men mentioned that their partners were nagging them to take dancing lessons.

And, just like that, Ben realised that he really had become part of the community. He'd been here a month, but it felt as if he'd been here for ever. He *belonged*.

Toni brought the goodies for the Tuesday

morning practice team meeting—a light, fluffy orange drizzle cake—and he handed her an envelope. 'Would you mind making a special delivery for me on the way to your reading class tomorrow, please?'

'To Jake? Of course. He'll be thrilled that you remembered his sticker,' she said.

'What's this?' Bill, one of the other doctors, asked.

'Jake Flowers. We'd both gone for a run on Sunday and ended up at the beach café,' Toni explained. 'Jake dislocated his elbow and Ben put it back into place.'

'Not just me. It was teamwork,' Ben said, 'because you and Archie kept him distracted so he didn't tense up.'

'That's what the practice is all about,' Ranjit said. 'Talking of teamwork—how's the new meal plan for the website coming along?'

'Is this Ranjit-speak for "bring samples"?' Toni teased.

He laughed. 'Yes, and in return I'll tweak my mum's recipe for *chana masala* for you.'

'Oh, now, I want samples of *that*,' Janice, one of the other doctors, said.

'We could have a practice pot-luck dinner,' Toni suggested. 'We each bring a dish, but we make sure we tweak it to suit diabetics or cardiac patients, and we use the recipes on the practice's website. Ranj, your garden's the biggest. Would you host it?'

'Done,' Ranjit said. 'We'll set a date and if we sort out between us beforehand who's doing mains, who's doing sides and who's doing dessert, it won't be like the antenatal pot-luck lunch I once went to when every single person brought tuna pasta salad!'

The team at his last practice hadn't really socialised much outside work, apart from the annual Christmas lunch, Ben thought. Here at Great Crowmell, it was very different. And he really, really liked it.

On Wednesday, Toni sent him a text suggesting lunch by the harbour when he'd finished morning surgery and she'd finished her reading session. And he thoroughly enjoyed sitting on the harbour wall, looking at the boats and the salt marshes, while they ate their wraps from the deli.

'Jake was absolutely thrilled that you remembered his sticker,' Toni told him.

'Good. It's important to keep promises to children,' he said. 'How's his arm?'

'Absolutely fine. Apparently it was a bit sore on Monday. But he told his teacher about Archie's wonderful jokes, and everyone in the class wanted to hear them—so I'm going to need some new ones before I run out. And, as you were so good, I'm going to beg for a couple of new ones from you every Tuesday from now until the end of term.'

'I have friends who work in Paediatrics,' he said. 'I'll get some from them so you've got a stock.'

'Brilliant,' she said.

Friends and colleagues.

That was what they'd agreed.

And they had a great working relationship.

Except Toni wanted more. He'd really come out of his shell over the last few weeks and become part of the heart of the community. Was he finally ready to move on from the heartbreak of his past? Or should she back off and give him more space? Was she just making the same mistake over again— except this time she'd chosen someone lovely but unobtainable, instead of having surface charm that hid the kind of man she didn't want? Would he ever let anyone close—and, if so would it be her?

So many unanswered questions.

And there was nothing she could do to change things. She just had to be patient.

Which she was finding more and more difficult to do.

Part way through Friday afternoon she had a phone call that left her reeling. 'Hey, Julia. How are you? Do you need one of the team to come out to see a resident?' she asked when Moira put the call through.

'No. I'm sorry, I've got some bad news for you. Because she was such a close family friend and you made a point of spending time with her every week, even on the days she wasn't well…' Julia dragged in a breath. 'I'm afraid there isn't a way to cushion this. Ginny passed away in her sleep last night.'

Ginny, her grandmother's best friend, had been almost a second grandmother when Toni had been growing up, and the news brought back all the sense of loss Toni had felt when Betty had died.

'Thank you for telling me,' she said. 'I'll call her son later to give my condolences to her family.' It was hard on the staff, too, when a resident died. 'And I'm sorry for your loss, as well.'

'Thank you. I just wanted to tell you the news myself today, as I knew you were fond of Ginny.'

'I was. She was fond of Archie, too. She always smiled when we walked in.'

'I know. I'd better let you get on. I'm sorry it's sad news.'

Toni held herself together for the rest of her shift. Her next patient was a teenager who had been having chest pains that his mother thought might be due to exam stress, but Toni gave him an X-ray to check that there wasn't an underlying problem that hadn't been diagnosed yet; thankfully, it was normal.

'I think your mum is probably right—the more worried you get, the more your muscles can tense up as part of the "fight or flight" response. That's why you feel a bit sweaty and dizzy as well, Darren,' she explained. 'Exercise can help—swimming, cycling, going for a walk—because it helps release tension and it gets your brain to produce serotonin. I can give you some websites with some online courses that could help you.'

'So it's not my heart?' Darren asked.

'It's not your heart,' she confirmed. 'But I'd like to see you in a couple of weeks to see how you're getting on and if your symptoms are any better. If they're not, we can try some medication to help with the symptoms. Avoiding caffeine can help, too—caffeine can disrupt your sleep and speed up your heartbeat, and when you're tired it's hard to control any anxious feelings. So switch to decaf coffee and herbal tea, and stay away from energy drinks and fizzy drinks.'

He bit his lip. 'But I need the energy drinks to help me concentrate for my exams.'

'Getting enough sleep will help you concentrate more,' she said. 'Try a warm bath before bed, or a hot milky drink, putting a bit of lavender on your pillow. It's worth having a look at different things to help you relax— and make sure you switch your phone or any other screen to night mode so the blue light doesn't affect your sleep.'

'Mum says I shouldn't look at a screen for an hour before bed,' Darren said.

'That would be preferable,' Toni said, 'but at this time of year it'll probably worry you more if you don't read things before bed. See what you can manage, and we'll review everything in a fortnight. Though obviously if you get chest pains again and they're worse, it's worth calling in to the emergency department for more tests.'

She booked him in on her computer, saw a couple of patients for smear tests, a couple more for blood pressure checks, and yet more

for their regular six-monthly medication re-
views—and then finally her shift was over.

She finished typing up her notes, made
sure her desk was clear, then took a deep
breath and walked out of the door.

Ginny's death had really knocked Toni
for six. Right at that moment it was hard
to put one foot in front of the other. Hard
to breathe. She missed her grandmother so
much—Betty's warmth, the way she had of
putting a positive spin on everything, the
way she could always make things better
with a hug. Losing Ginny brought back all
the sadness of losing her grandmother.

And right now Toni knew she was letting
her grandmother down by moping and being
miserable. Ginny was at peace, now, no longer lost in a world of confusion and fear. Plus
Toni knew that she and Archie had helped
to bring a bright spot in Ginny's last days.

Find the bright side. Toni could almost
hear her grandmother's voice echoing in her
head.

Although there didn't feel as if there was
a bright side.

One foot in front of the other, she told
herself. But, as she walked down the cor-

ridor, her vision was blurred by tears, and she stumbled.

'Toni? Are you—? No. Stupid question. Of course you're not all right,' Ben said.

She hadn't even noticed him in the corridor. 'I'm fine,' she lied.

'You're crying,' he said gently, 'and your eyes are puffy enough for me to know you've been crying for a while. You're not fine at all. Look, why don't you come back with me? I'll make you a cup of tea—and you can stay for dinner. You don't have to talk. I'll give you space.'

His kindness broke her. 'Archie…'

'Will be fine and he won't mind waiting a little bit longer for his dinner,' he said firmly. 'I'll drop you home after we've eaten. Did you drive in this morning?'

'No, I walked,' she said.

'Then that makes things easy. Come on.'

He drove her back to his house, keeping the radio on low. Just as he'd promised, he didn't push her to make meaningless small talk—or, worse still, spill what was in her heart. He made her a cup of tea that was way too strong and too sweet, but she drank it anyway, recognising the fact that he was trying to comfort her and not wanting to make him feel awkward.

And it did help. Just knowing that he was there, understanding that she felt bad, and he was taking care of her in a practical way by cooking her dinner and making her a drink—with no pressure to talk until she was ready. He didn't even push her to talk when he served dinner at his kitchen table.

'Take one mouthful,' he coaxed. 'Just one mouthful and you'll feel better. I promise.'

She forced herself to take a mouthful. And another. And then somehow she'd managed to clear her plate.

'Thank you,' she said. 'That was really good. And you were right. It did help.'

Unlike Sean, Ben didn't gloat about being proved right. He just gave her one of those almost shy smiles that made her heart do a backflip. 'Any time.'

'I'll do the washing up.'

He shook his head. 'There isn't much. I'll do it later. I think right now you need a hug.'

'I do,' she admitted.

And how good it felt to have the warmth of his arms enveloping her, the clean citrus scent of his shower gel filling her senses.

'Talk to me, Toni,' he said softly. 'Tell me

what's in your head, even if it's a jumble. Let it out. It's not going any further than me, I promise. And maybe saying it out loud will help.'

She closed her eyes and rested her head on his shoulder. 'Ginny died—one of the residents at The Beeches.'

'The one who doesn't talk?'

'Yes. She was my gran's best friend. She lived just round the corner, and she was like a second gran to me and Stacey. We used to go to hers from school if Gran was at work, and she helped us when Gran was first ill. Then she got ill, too. I know I should be glad that she's at peace now instead of being lost and confused, but…' Her words trailed off.

'It's brought back the loss of your grandmother?' he guessed.

'Yes. And Ginny was sort of the last link to her.'

His arms tightened around her, and she was seriously grateful that he understood her so well.

'That's hard,' he said.

'I miss her, Ben. I miss my mum and my dad.' Then she remembered when she'd talked to Sean about it and how dismissive he'd been. 'I'll pull myself together. Just ignore me. I'm being boring and selfish.'

'It's not selfish or boring at all,' he said. 'You're allowed to feel, Toni. You're allowed to grieve.'

So very different from the way that Sean had seen things.

'In the weeks I've known you I've seen for myself that you're one of the nicest, kindest, most unselfish women I've met. Don't be so hard on yourself.'

He meant it. And it did actually make her feel better, knowing he understood how she felt and wasn't judging her as harshly as she judged herself. 'Gran always taught me to look on the bright side.'

'She was right. There's always a bright side. Sometimes you have to look really hard for it, but it's there.'

'I know. I'm being wet.'

'No. You're human,' he said gently.

She willed the tears to stay back, not wanting to howl her eyes out in front of him.

She had no idea how long they stood there, just holding each other; but then somehow his cheek was against hers, and she was remembering how it felt to dance with him, and then her mouth was touching the corner of his lips. The next thing she knew, they were kissing—really kissing—and it felt as if he'd just lit touch-paper.

They were both shaking when he broke the kiss, and he looked stricken. Guilty.

'Toni, I'm sorry. I shouldn't have done that. I don't want to take advantage of you.'

'You're not. I think I started it.' She couldn't help laying her palm against his cheek, and he twisted his head so he could press a kiss into her hand.

'I just wanted to make you feel better, the way you did for me when I had a tough day,' he said.

'You have. You fed me. You got me to put one foot in front of the other and move, and I really appreciate it.'

His sea-green eyes were almost black, his pupils were so huge.

And she couldn't resist reaching up to steal another kiss.

He looked haunted. 'Toni. This isn't fair of me. Neither of us is in a place to start a relationship.'

'I know. But right now,' she said, 'I need to celebrate life.'

This was a really bad idea.

His head knew he ought to find an excuse,

something that wouldn't make her feel bad. Right now she was vulnerable, grieving— and this was a knee-jerk reaction, a need to make herself feel alive while she was facing the grim reality of death.

He wasn't going to take advantage of her, even though his heart was screaming out to him to kiss her, make her feel better, make them *both* feel better.

Then she laid her palm against his cheek again. 'I need you, Ben,' she whispered. 'Make it better. Please.'

And then he was lost.

How could he say no? How could he leave her miserable and hurting?

'Are you sure about this?' he asked, while his common sense was still just about clinging on.

'Very sure,' she said.

And then there was only one thing Ben could do: to dip his head again and brush his mouth against Toni's. Softly. Gently. A kiss of warmth and promise.

Then he repeated it again, this time taking a tiny nibble of her lower lip, coaxing her into a response. When she slid her fingers into his hair and kissed him back, he relaxed, knowing this was going to be all right.

She broke the kiss.

'If you change your mind at any point, that's OK. Because I've never bullied a woman in my life before and I'm not going to start now.'

She reached up and stole a kiss back. 'Thank you.'

He wanted to behave like a caveman and his pulse was leaping crazily. 'Except I don't have a condom.'

'I do,' she said. 'In my handbag.' She fetched it and took his hand. 'Take me to bed, Ben,' she whispered.

The look in her eyes made him so dizzy with desire that he could barely think straight. But he lifted her hand, pressed a kiss into her palm and folded her fingers over it.

'Come with me,' he whispered back, and led her up the stairs to his bedroom. He closed the curtains and snapped on the bedside light; then he pulled her back into his arms and kissed her lingeringly.

She was still wearing her nurse practitioner's uniform of navy trousers and a navy tunic with white piping. With shaking hands, he undid the buttons of her tunic and discovered that she was wearing a lacy bra.

'That's one hell of a view,' he said, his voice husky with wanting her.

'Thank you.' She dipped her head in acknowledgement.

He slid the tunic off her shoulders and hung it neatly over the back of the chair; then he unzipped her trousers and let them slide to the floor so she could step out of them.

'You're wearing too much. We need to do something about that,' she said.

He smiled. 'I'm in your hands.'

'Good.'

She undid his tie and then the buttons of his shirt, very slowly, one by one. He could feel the pads of her fingertips stroking the skin of his abdomen, warm and soft and very, very sure of what she was doing; it made him catch his breath as a wave of desire surged through him.

She unbuttoned his trousers and nudged the material over his hips so they fell to the floor; he stepped out of them, he dipped his head again and brushed his mouth lightly against hers in the sweetest, gentlest kiss. Within a nanosecond the kiss had turned so hot that his bones felt as though they were melting.

She was shaking when he broke the kiss.

'The way you make me feel—it's like when you dance with me, as if I'm walking on air,' she whispered. She rubbed the pad of her thumb along his lower lip. 'You're beautiful. Everything about you.'

Desire licked down his spine. 'That's how you make me feel, too.' He traced the lacy edge of her bra with the tip of one finger. 'Just gorgeous. You blow my mind.'

He slid the straps of her bra off her shoulders, kissing her bare skin before unsnapping her bra and letting it fall to the floor between them, then dropped to his knees and teased her with his hands and his lips and his tongue, stroking her skin and kissing her until she was quivering.

And then it was her turn to touch him, to kneel down next to him and let her fingertips skate over his pectorals and down over his abdomen, taking it slowly and deliberately, learning the texture of his skin with her fingertips and just how and where he liked being touched.

'My turn again,' he whispered, and did the same to her.

Then he picked her up, pushed the duvet to one side and laid her down against the soft pillows. He kissed his way down her body, paying attention to all the hidden parts: the curve of her elbow, the soft undersides of her breasts, until she was murmuring with pleasure.

Then he knelt back and worked his way upwards from her ankles, touching and kissing and nuzzling until she tipped her head back against the pillows and fisted her hands in his hair.

'Ben, this is killing me,' she murmured.

He wanted this first time to be for her; so he teased her with his mouth and his hands, stoking the waves of pleasure until her climax finally hit and she cried out.

When he shifted up the bed to lie beside her, she curved her fingers round his shaft, stroking and caressing until he arched against the bed and gasped with pleasure.

Then she undid the little foil packet and rolled the condom over his shaft, then shifted to straddle him.

'Now,' she said, and lowered herself onto him.

'Toni,' he breathed, and pushed up to meet her.

She felt amazing.

He laced his fingers through hers as she moved over him.

This should've been awkward and a bit clumsy; instead, it felt so right. Perfect. He was completely in tune with her, in a way he'd never expected.

As he felt her body tightening round his, he released her hands, sat up and wrapped his arms tightly round her.

Their climaxes hit at the same time, and he jammed his mouth over hers.

She kissed him back, wrapping her arms just as tightly round him.

As the aftershocks of his climax died away, he lay back and let her climb off him.

'I need to deal with the condom,' he said. 'Don't go anywhere.'

When he came back to bed, he wrapped her in his arms.

'Sorry. I didn't mean to...' Her breath shuddered.

'You have absolutely nothing to be sorry for,' Ben said, stroking her face.

'Apart from abandoning my dog.'

'You've just made him wait a little bit longer for his dinner. And he loves you so he won't hold it against you,' he said. 'I would ask you to stay, but is there anyone who could feed Archie and let him out?'

She grimaced. 'I need to go home.'

'OK. I'll drive you home now.'

'Sorry. I feel as if I'm being selfish and ungrateful and—'

He cut off her words by kissing her. 'Stop apologising. We can think about this and overanalyse it another time. Right now, you need comfort. Help yourself to whatever you need in the bathroom.'

'Thank you.'

While she sorted herself out in the bathroom, Ben got dressed; and then he drove her back to her cottage.

'Thank you for bringing me home. Would you like to come in for a cup of tea?' she asked.

Was she simply being polite and hoping that he'd refuse? Or did she really want his company but also didn't want to impose on him by asking him to stay?

The sadness in her grey eyes decided him. 'I'd love a cup of tea.'

Archie greeted them ecstatically when they walked into the kitchen.

'I'll make the tea while you sort out his dinner and what have you,' Ben said.

'Thank you.' She let the dog out and re-filled his water and food bowls. Archie scoffed his dinner in what seemed like three seconds flat, then came to sit at Toni's feet, curling in close to her as if he recognised that she needed comfort.

'Is there anyone you need to call?' Ben asked, placing the mug of tea in front of her.

'No. I'll text Stacey in the morning. Thank you.'

'Is that photograph on the fridge of your grandmother?' he asked, gesturing to the snap of a middle-aged woman standing next to a sandcastle on the beach, with a much younger Toni and Stacey.

'Yes. I would have been about six and Stacey was eight at the time. It's one of my favourites.' She smiled. 'So many happy memories.'

And bittersweet, because they couldn't be shared with her grandmother, he guessed.

'I learned baking at her knee, too,' Toni told him. 'I loved my mum dearly—like Stacey, she was amazing with a needle and she was a costume designer for one of the West End theatres. But when it came to cooking, it was legendary that my mum could burn water. My dad had to do all the cooking, and he wasn't that brilliant at it, either.' Her mouth curved. 'We ate a lot of sausages, chips and baked beans. And salad. It was one of the reasons we always loved coming to Gran's—it meant we got perfect roast dinners and home-made apple crumble with proper custard.'

It made Ben feel slightly guilty that he'd pushed his family away, of late. He had something that Toni clearly missed so badly, yet he'd taken it for granted. 'It sounds great.'

Toni smiled. 'Gran would have liked you.' Though she hadn't liked Sean, saying that he was too full of himself. Toni had told herself that it was simply a case of them rubbing each other up the wrong way—but eventually Betty had been proved absolutely right about Sean.

'I'm sorry,' Ben said softly, 'that you've lost so much in your life.'

'It happens,' she said. 'And I'm trying to focus on the fact that I did at least have a good relationship with my parents, my gran and Ginny, even if I didn't have them for as long as I would have liked. Not everyone's that lucky.'

That was true. Ben's own parents weren't good at the emotional stuff and they hadn't known how to support him when Karen had dropped her bombshell. But he loved them, and he loved his sister—and Toni had made him realise it was time to make more of an effort instead of taking them all for granted.

'Just remember that you and Archie helped to make Ginny's life happier in her last few months,' he said.

'I know. It's still going to be hard, walking in there on Monday afternoon.'

'I'll go with you, if you want me to arrange cover for my shift,' he said.

She shook her head. 'Thank you, but I need to pull myself together and face this.'

He went over to her chair and wrapped his arms around her. 'OK. But I'll cook for you on Monday night, or we can go to a dog-friendly pub with Archie and have dinner, so you don't have to worry about cooking.'

'That's kind,' she said.

He didn't feel kind, where she was concerned.

He felt all kinds of things that he was still trying to get his head round.

They spent the rest of the evening on the sofa, with the dog curled up between them, watching reruns of old comedy shows on television. When Toni started yawning, Ben kissed her forehead. 'I'd better let you get some sleep.'

'Ben—I know it's a lot to ask, but would you stay tonight?' she asked.

Spend the whole night with her.

Just to comfort her? Or was this the next step, heralding a change in their relationship—a move from friends to lovers to dating properly?

And was he ready to move on from the past?

Then again, even if he wasn't, how could he resist the entreaty in her face? She clearly didn't want to be alone. He knew how that felt.

'OK. I'll stay,' he said softly.

CHAPTER SEVEN

BEN WOKE WHEN sunlight filtered through the cotton curtains. He was spooned against Toni, with his arms wrapped around her; it would be oh, so easy to close his eyes again and go back to sleep. Except he had a shift at the surgery this morning and he needed to get up.

He also needed to talk to Toni, but that would have to wait until later today. It wasn't a conversation he wanted to rush.

This was the first time he'd woken in bed with someone since he'd split up with Karen. The first time for years that he'd woken in bed with someone other than Karen. In some ways, it felt strange and uncomfortable; in others, it felt good—because it was Toni. He liked her. A lot. He liked her warmth, the way she always saw the good in things. His world had felt a lot brighter since she'd been in it.

He kissed her shoulder. 'Toni. Wake up.'

'Hmm?' She shifted around to face him and her grey eyes widened in apparent surprise; and then she smiled at him, clearly remembering last night. 'Good morning.'

'I'm due at the surgery,' he said, 'so I need to go home and change.'

'Of course.'

He tucked a strand of hair behind her ear. How soft and silky it was. 'Can I see you this afternoon? Maybe we could take Archie for a run on the beach.' He paused. 'And talk.'

'That would be good.'

'See you outside Scott's Café at two?'

'I'll be there,' she promised. 'Can I get you some breakfast before you go?'

He glanced at the clock on the bedside table. 'Thanks, but I need to get going. I have to be at the surgery by half-past eight.'

'OK.' She stroked his face. 'Thank you for staying last night.'

'No problem.' He paused. 'Are you OK?'

'I will be,' she said. 'And you have patients to see. They're more important.'

Typical Toni, not putting herself first. He stole a kiss. 'They're not more important than you, but I do have to go. I'll see you later. Close your eyes.'

She laughed. 'Because your clothes are in a heap on my floor? In the circumstances—'

'—I shouldn't be shy,' he finished. 'Weirdly, I am.'

'Then I'll close my eyes, shy boy,' she teased.

Ben climbed out of bed and dressed swiftly. 'See you at two,' he said.

'I'll see you out. I need to let Archie out anyway.' She looked at him. 'What's sauce for the goose is sauce for the gander, you know.'

'I'll see you in the kitchen,' he said.

Which meant he was the one to get the canine greeting of a slow tail thump, a luxuriant stretch as Archie climbed out of his basket, and a wet nose shoved against his hand to say hello.

A month ago, he would have flinched and moved away from the dog.

Now, enjoying the experience, he scratched behind the dog's ears. 'Good morning, Archie.'

Archie licked him in greeting, and Ben smiled.

Toni joined him a few moments later, clad

in a short fluffy dressing gown. 'Are you sure I can't get you coffee and toast to go?' she asked.

'I'm sure. I'll grab a banana and a coffee at the surgery,' he said, and kissed her lightly. 'See you later.'

Ben Mitchell was definitely on the side of the angels, Toni thought as he closed the front door behind him. He'd helped her to function yesterday when grief had sideswiped her. He'd stayed, last night, when she'd needed someone to hold her.

So where did they go from here?

He'd said that they needed to talk, and he was right.

The night of the dance, he'd kissed her and they'd both backed away, both panicked by their pasts. But the attraction between them was still there, and it wasn't going away any time soon. It wasn't just a physical thing. She liked him. More than liked him. And she rather thought it was mutual, or else he would either have made an excuse not to stay last night, or persuaded her to go and stay with her sister.

She'd barely dated since she'd split up with Sean; there just hadn't been the spark with the few men she'd gone out with, and they'd agreed to keep things platonic. And she knew Ben hadn't dated since his ex had left. Was he really ready to take a risk with her?

Their conversation that afternoon needed to be frank and honest, even if it hurt. They needed to know what each other wanted; trying to second-guess would only make things harder.

She called Stacey with the news about Ginny—leaving out Ben's involvement—and then called next door to see if Shona needed anything, caught up with all her chores, and was sitting with Archie outside Scott's Café at five minutes to two.

Ben had changed into jeans, a T-shirt and running shoes, topped with a pair of sunglasses. He looked absolutely gorgeous and Toni's heart skipped a beat.

'Hi.'

Was he going to greet her with a kiss?

Her stomach clenched with disappointment when he didn't.

OK. So this was obviously going to be a 'Dear Jane' conversation. He'd tell her that he was the one at fault, not her, and he'd ask her to cool things between them back to their previous professional relationship.

She braced herself. 'Shall we go?' she asked brightly.

'Sure.'

She waited until they were on the designated part of the beach before she let Archie off the lead. Though that meant she didn't really have anything to do with her hands, once she'd put Archie's lead into her beach bag.

Ben still hadn't said anything, so she was guessing that he was trying to find a nice way of telling her that he didn't want to take their relationship further.

When they got to the dunes, he said, 'Hydration break?'

Which was just what they'd done the day he'd had the case that had brought his past back to haunt him. 'Sure. I brought an extra bottle of water.'

'And I brought strawberries,' he said. 'They're washed and hulled. And grown locally.'

'For a moment I thought you were going to say you picked them yourself.'

'Not quite. I picked them up from the farm shop on the way back from work,' he said.

'OK.' How horrible that they were reduced to small talk. But she didn't know what else to do. 'Did you have a good shift?'

'Yes. Did you have a good morning?' he asked, equally polite.

'Yes.'

He took her hand and laced his fingers between hers.

Here it comes, she thought. *It's not you, it's me...*

She couldn't bear it. She would rather be the one to call it quits, the one to walk away. 'I'm sorry about last night,' she said.

'Don't apologise. You were upset. Of course I wasn't going to just leave you on your own. I'm glad I could be there for you.'

'As my friend.'

'That's why we need to talk,' he said softly.

'I understand. You're not ready for—'

Ben cut off the rest of her words by kissing her.

Once she was stunned into silence, he said, 'I wasn't expecting this thing between us. I thought I was still licking my wounds after Karen. But there's something about you I can't resist, Toni. I know it's not fair of me to ask you to start dating me properly. I'm still working things through in my head. But the feelings I have towards you just aren't going away.' He paused. 'But it's your call. I know you've been hurt before. But I would never give you an ultimatum like Sean did. I'd never want you to stop being who you are. I'm not like your ex, and I know you're not like mine. Do you think we could give it a go?'

She felt her eyes widen. 'Are you...asking me out?'

He nodded. 'I feel as if I'm fifteen years old again, not thirty-five. I'm terrified you're going to say no—and I'm also terrified that you're going to say yes and I'm going to make a mess of it.'

'You already know I have a habit of picking Mr Wrong,' she said. 'With the good guys, there's no chemistry.'

'I think there's chemistry between us,' he said softly.

'That's why this whole thing is so confusing. You're not like the men I usually date—and I wasn't looking to start dating someone.'

'So we both think this might be a mistake,' he said.

She nodded. 'Except you're right. There's

chemistry between us, and it isn't going away any time soon.'

'So let's see how it goes,' he said. 'Maybe we should keep it just between us, for now, until we know what's happening.'

She grinned. 'It's pretty hard to keep things quiet in a small village. But OK. We'll see how it goes—and try to keep it just between us.'

'Good.' He leaned over and stole a kiss. 'So what sort of things do you like doing?'

'Apart from walking or running on the beach?' she asked. 'I like music. I'm hopeless at dancing, though.'

'You just need practice,' he said. 'How about the theatre? Cinema?'

'Yes to both, and anything from Shakespeare to stand up to sci-fi. Not gory stuff, though,' she said, 'or all-out weepies. You?'

'Same as you, and I prefer drama to comedy. I really hate slapstick,' he said. 'But I love bad puns.'

'How about sport?' she asked.

'I'd rather play than watch it,' he told her. 'You?'

'I'd rather not watch or play,' she said. 'Except for throwing tennis balls, if you can count that as sport.'

He grinned. 'And I'm guessing you get a fair bit of practice at that.'

'I do indeed.'

'Museums?' he asked.

'Yes. And art galleries,' she said. 'Especially if there's a nice café.'

'Maybe we can make a list of places we'd like to go,' he said.

'Good idea. My idea of the perfect day,' she said, 'is just taking Archie somewhere for a really long walk. It doesn't matter whether it's by the sea, in the forest or in a park.'

'That sounds good to me,' he said. 'So how about we go to the cinema tonight and take Archie exploring tomorrow?'

'That would be perfect,' she said with a smile. 'Let's walk a bit further.'

This time, they walked hand in hand. The tide was out, so it took a while to reach the sea; when they finally reached the shoreline, they both took off their shoes and paddled in the shallows, while Archie galloped through the water, splashing them both.

'Sorry,' she said.

He smiled. 'He's having fun. And so am I.'

'Me, too. Though we do need to keep an eye on the tide,' she said. 'Once it turns, it comes in fast—and if you're the wrong side of the channel you can get caught out.' She raised an eyebrow. 'I remember Stacey once went to the beach a couple of villages down with some of her mates, and they left their clothes on the sand while they went swimming— but they didn't leave their stuff far enough up the slope. The sea came in when they were too busy having fun to notice and washed all their clothes away.'

'As the tide's so fast, is there any kind of warning signal?' he asked.

'Yes. There's a siren,' she said.

'That's good to know.' He smiled at her. 'This place is amazing. I'm glad I moved here.'

'I have no regrets about moving back here from London,' she said.

They walked a bit further, then a teenager in a group at the edge of the water started yelling. 'My foot! It really hurts!'

'Are there jellyfish locally?' Ben asked.

'I haven't heard any reports so far this summer, but it's been warm enough for jelly-fish,' Toni said. 'Or maybe he might have stepped on broken glass or the sharp edge of a can.'

She whistled to Archie and they hurried

over to the teenagers, who were coming out of the water.

'I'm a doctor and Toni is a nurse practitioner. Can we help?' Ben asked. 'What happened?'

The boy was white-faced. 'I was just mucking about in the water, and something hurt my foot. It's *burning*.'

'Can we have a look?' Ben asked.

The boy nodded, and sat down; Ben sat down beside him and took a look at his foot. 'It doesn't look as if you've stood on glass or anything sharp, but there is a tiny spot of blood on your heel, which suggests to me it's some kind of puncture.'

'It feels as if it's burning,' the boy said again. 'All the way up my leg.'

'It might be weever fish,' Toni said. 'I haven't heard any reports of them for a while, but they bury themselves in the sand, and if you stand on them the spines are really sharp—plus they contain venom.' She grimaced. 'Sorry to tell you this, but if it was a weever fish the pain will get worse over the next half an hour.'

'It's bad enough now—I don't think I can walk on it,' the boy said, grimacing.

'We need to get the spines out of your foot.

Archie, sit,' she told the dog, who sat perfectly still while Toni rummaged in her bag. 'What's your name?' she asked the boy.

'Ollie,' he said.

'OK, Ollie. I've got tweezers in here. Can one of your mates run up to the lifeguards' hut and ask them to get some hot water ready? Tell them we think you stood on a weever fish. I'll get the spines out of your foot, Ollie, and we'll help you up to the lifeguard. But in the meantime I need you to talk to Ben about your medical history—any allergies, any medication.'

She busied herself taking the tiny spines out of Ollie's foot with the tweezers, while he told Ben that he wasn't on any medication, he was allergic to fabric plasters, and his foot really, really hurt.

'I'm going to have to squeeze your foot now to make it bleed, so the blood washes the venom out,' Toni said. 'I'm sorry. It might hurt a bit.'

Ollie clenched his fist. 'That's OK. Do it.'

He winced as she squeezed the puncture site, but didn't make a sound.

'What we'll do now is give you some paracetamol to help with the pain, and then we need to put your food in really hot water for half an hour,' Ben said. 'That will break down the poison and increase blood flow to the site of the sting, to help it heal.'

'So my mates aren't going to have to pee on my foot or anything?' Ollie asked.

'No,' Ben reassured him, 'and you don't need to put vinegar on it, either. You're best not covering up the wound, because that could risk the puncture getting infected.'

'You'll be fine by tomorrow. If you find the area around the site really swells up, your chest hurts or you can't breathe properly, or you feel lightheaded or start throwing up, you need to go straight to hospital or ring for an ambulance,' Toni said.

'And keep an eye on the wound—not just for swelling. If it gets redder or there's any sign of pus, come straight to the surgery and we'll give you some antibiotics,' Ben said.

'Got it,' Ollie said. 'And thank you for helping. You're not even on duty.'

'It's all part of being a medic,' Ben said. 'You never just leave people when you can help.'

They helped Ollie walk back towards the

lifeguard station, and his friends met them halfway back.

'The lifeguards are getting the hot water ready,' one of them said. He looked at Toni and Ben. 'And I told them you're a doctor and a nurse.'

'Archie isn't allowed on that side of the beach,' Toni said, 'so I can't go any further with you.'

'I'll go to the lifeguards with Ollie and fill them in,' Ben said. 'See you at the café?'

'Good idea. All the best, Ollie.' She patted the teenager's shoulder.

'Thanks again for helping me. Even if it did hurt,' he said.

'No problem. Take care,' Toni said.

Ben came into the café twenty minutes later. 'It looks as if he'll be fine. He knows to look out for signs of complications.'

'Just as well we were there,' Toni said.

'Yes.' Ben made a fuss of Archie. 'Do you want a coffee or something cold?'

'Coffee would be great, thanks.'

There was a soft woof from Archie and Ben laughed. 'I'm sure you'd love a sausage, but I bet you've already had one today.'

'He has and, even though he was brilliantly behaved while we were treating Ollie, he's not having another or he'll get fat,' Toni said firmly.

'Tomorrow,' Ben promised the dog in a stage whisper.

When he returned with a coffee, they pored over the screen on his phone to see what was showing at the local cinemas.

'There's a pop-up cinema in the grounds of the local stately home,' Ben said. 'I quite like the idea of watching a film outdoors. If we can get tickets, shall we go?'

'*Mamma Mia*. I love that film.' She smiled. 'Are you sure it's not too girly for you?'

'It'll be fun. I haven't been to an outdoor cinema in years,' he said.

A couple of minutes later, their tickets were booked.

'The website says there are food stalls, so all you need to bring are fold-up chairs or a blanket to sit on,' he said.

'I have some fold-up chairs and blankets, as long as you don't mind a few dog hairs on them.'

He laughed. 'I don't mind dog hairs. So if I pick you up at seven, we've got plenty of time to set up our chairs, have something to eat, and then enjoy the show,' he said.

'Sounds perfect. See you at seven,' she said.

* * *

At seven, Ben walked up the path to Toni's door. He wasn't sure whether he felt more nervous, excited or scared. All three at once, maybe. Even though he and Toni were colleagues and had become friends, this was their first official date. The first time for the best part of a decade that he'd dated someone who wasn't Karen. He wasn't even sure that he remembered any of the etiquette of dating. When to hold her hand, when to kiss her. What to wear, even: was he dressed right? Too formal, too casual? He'd opted for jeans and a light sweater, given that they were spending the evening outdoors. Would Toni think he was taking her for granted and not making an effort to dress up in something a bit smarter?

It felt as if he was fifteen again, gauche and shy. Which was crazy.

Why was he making such a big deal of this? Toni was lovely. Or maybe that was why: because he suspected that she could matter. A lot.

He pulled himself together and knocked on Toni's door. She answered, wearing a pretty top, a skirt and high heels. She looked absolutely gorgeous and his mouth went dry from pure desire. He couldn't actually speak, for a moment, and had to clear his throat. *Idiot*, he told himself. *Speak to her.* 'You look—' He stopped, unable to find the right words. He didn't want her to think he was gushing, but he also wanted to tell her how beautiful she looked. 'You look fabulous,' he said, knowing it sounded lame.

'Thank you.' She grinned, suddenly looking younger herself. 'So do you.'

Funny how it made him feel more relaxed. 'Thank you. Are you going to be warm enough?' he asked. 'Once the sun goes down, it will be chilly, especially as we won't be moving about.'

'I have blankets to snuggle under,' she said, indicating the bag by her side. 'And two fold-up chairs.'

'Brilliant. Let's go.' He took the chairs and the blankets from her and carried them to his car, then drove to the stately home in the next village. The car park was full; clearly the pop-up cinema was popular and they'd been lucky to get tickets.

Once they'd found a place to set up the chairs, they queued for pizza and hot chocolate. 'The food's my treat,' she said, 'because you bought the cinema tickets.'

'It's our first date,' he said, 'so shouldn't this be my treat—especially as it was my idea?'

'Which century are you living in, Dr Mitchell?' she teased, giving him a sassy grin.

'Point taken,' he said dryly. 'And thank you.'

Although the film wasn't really his thing, Ben enjoyed sitting under the stars with Toni, with a fleecy blanket tucked round them and her fingers twined through his. It had been years since he'd last held hands with someone at the cinema and he was surprised by how happy something so simple and so small made him feel.

'Thank you. I really enjoyed tonight,' she said when he dropped her home and walked her to her front door.

'Me, too.' He kissed her softly. 'Can I see you tomorrow?'

'I'd like that.'

'Let's go somewhere we can take Archie,' he said.

'That'd be brilliant.' She paused. 'Um—I…'

'It's our first official date,' he said, 'so I'm just going to kiss you goodnight.'

She stole a kiss. 'I like your old-fashioned courtesy. Even though it kind of makes our relationship the wrong way round.'

'Spending the night together before we started dating?' he asked.

She groaned. 'Does that make me a bit of a tart?'

He wrapped his arms around her. 'No. You're lovely. But I want to do this properly now. I want us to get to know each other better before we go to bed together again.'

'To be sure we're doing the right thing?' At his nod, she said, 'Me, too.' She kissed him. 'See you tomorrow. I'll have a think about where we can go.'

In the end, they took a picnic and went further down the coast to Brancaster.

'It's like Great Crowmell in that the tide comes in really quickly, and a few people have been stranded while they were exploring the wreck,' she told him. 'But as long as we keep an eye on the sea, we'll be fine.'

The beach stretched for miles, and Ben really enjoyed walking hand in hand with Toni, barefoot in the warm shallow water, with the dog splashing about in front of them.

There was something magical about the

place, with the bright blue sky contrasting sharply with the pale golden sand, and the light of the sun on the waves lapping against the shoreline looked almost like fairy dust.

After Karen had left, Ben had been so sure he'd never get involved with anyone, let alone fall in love. But here, on the gentle East Anglian coast, he felt different—because Toni was beside him. Right now, the world felt filled with brightness and hope, an adventure to revel in.

And every moment of the day felt special—everything from the warmth and brightness in Toni's grey eyes, through to the fun of finding pretty shells on the beach, buying ice creams from the kiosk by the car park and sharing a picnic on the dunes. Ben couldn't remember when he'd last felt this carefree—this *happy*.

When the tide started to come in, they headed back to the car.

'I've had such a great day,' he said. 'And I know it's selfish of me, but I'm not ready for it to end just yet.'

'Me neither,' she admitted.

When she met his gaze, it felt as if his heart had exploded

'Toni.' He stroked her face, then rubbed the pad of his thumb along her lower lip. She caught his thumb gently between her teeth, and his pulse kicked up a notch. He leaned forward and kissed her, and it felt as if fireworks were going off around him, massive starbursts full of joy.

When he broke the kiss, he was trembling. And so was she.

'I want to show you something,' she said.

He nodded, and she drove them further up the coast.

The sun was starting to slip down the sky.

'I thought this was the east coast so you'd see the sun rise over the sea?' Ben said.

'This is the only west-facing beach in Norfolk. The sunsets here are amazing,' Toni said. 'Stacey and I used to love it when Gran took us here. I wanted to share it with you.'

They found a space on a bench on the cliff top and watched the sun slide lower. The huge red ball cast a plume of red light across the silvery blue sea, and Ben slid his arm around Toni, with Archie curled by their feet.

'I used to like watching the sunset from Primrose Hill when I was in London,' Ben said. 'You had the whole city spread out in front of you with all the amazing colours in the sky. But this is amazing.' It wasn't just the romance of the sunset, though. *She* made him feel amazing.

'Do you miss London?' she asked.

'I grew up there, so I do miss it a bit,' he admitted. 'But I'm coming to love Great Crowmell. The people, the place, and it's wonderful to live so near to the sea.' He looked at her. 'My sister's coming to visit, the weekend after next.'

'Uh-huh.'

'I was wondering if maybe you'd like to meet her.'

Her eyes were very clear. 'As your colleague?'

'Or as my girlfriend.' The words were out before he could stop them.

Her eyes widened. 'So we'd be official.'

This was it. The moment to prove to himself that he could move on, 'Official,' he said.

And her answering smile made the world feel full of wonder.

CHAPTER EIGHT

Monday was hard for Toni, walking into a building full of memories.

Ben sent her a text at lunchtime.

Thinking of you this afternoon. Here if you need me.

Toni had no intention of calling him, knowing that he would be busy seeing patients; but she really appreciated his support.

When she arrived, everyone at The Beeches was subdued, and even Archie couldn't get a smile out of Julia.

'Days like these, I hate my job,' Julia said.

'Hey,' Toni said, giving her a hug. 'You've made a real difference to the residents' lives. You've got nothing to reproach yourself for.'

'And death goes with the territory, I know. It's like when you work in the emergency department and you know you can't save everyone, no matter how hard you work and how much effort you put in.'

'I brought you these from my garden,' Toni said, handing her a bunch of golden roses. 'These were Gran's favourite. And they smell amazing.'

'Bless you. Sunshine in a vase,' Julia said.

The residents were all talking about Ginny, all missing her; though petting Archie seemed to help some of them relax a bit more. After her therapy dog session at the nursing home, Toni took Archie for a run on the beach before heading back to her house, needing the endorphins to lift her mood. Ben had left her a second text.

Hope things were bearable. Let me know when you want me to pick you up. Dinner at a dog-friendly pub or I'll cook for you.

She called him. 'Hi. I'm home.'

'How are you doing?' he asked.

'A little bit sad,' she admitted. 'Julia gave me a photograph that one of the staff had taken of Ginny with Archie, a few months back.'

'That's nice. Something to hold onto—

good memories,' he said. 'When do you want me to pick you up?'

'To be honest, I don't really want to go anywhere,' she said. 'I'm not quite in the mood for socialising.'

'Then I'll bring dinner to you, if you don't mind me taking over your kitchen. Half an hour?' he suggested.

'That'd be nice,' she said.

She splashed her face with water. Ben was so much more thoughtful than any of her exes had been. Sean couldn't cook, so he would've demanded to go out for dinner—and he would've sulked at her refusal. Ben completely understood how she felt and he'd come up with a perfect compromise.

Why on earth had Ben's ex fallen for someone else? Toni wondered. She couldn't understand it. If he had some deep character flaw, it would've shown up by now. Even the most practised charmer couldn't keep up the pretence all the time, and Ben wasn't a charmer. He was genuine.

He turned up with an armful of sweet-scented stocks. 'It's a kind of cheer-you-up thing,' he explained.

'Thank you. They're my favourites. I love the scent.'

'I'm glad you like them.' He gave her the cheekiest wink. 'I thought the in-your-face pink ones would be perfect for you.'

'Because I'm loud?'

'Because you're bright and lovely,' he corrected, and kissed her lightly. 'Right. Dinner is in ten minutes.'

'Seriously? What did you do, buy fresh pasta and a jar of sauce?'

'Yes to the fresh pasta,' he said, 'and it's from the deli, so I know it's the good stuff. No to the sauce. By the time you've got those flowers in water, dinner will be almost done.'

'Can I do anything to help?'

'Put the salad into a bowl,' he said.

By the time she'd arranged the stocks in a vase, and shaken the bag of salad leaves and the tomatoes into bowls, dinner was ready.

'It smells amazing,' she said.

'Scallops and linguini in garlic and lemon sauce,' he said. 'A nice recipe for our diabetics, if you take out the Parmesan.'

She tasted a forkful. 'You could've been a chef. I think you'd give the posh Michelin-starred place at Little Crowmell a run for its money.'

'Thank you. I've just always liked cooking,' he said. 'It relaxes me. I'm planning a barbecue for when my sister and her family come to stay.'

'I'll make pudding,' she said. 'What do they all like?'

'I do know Jessie will do anything for cheesecake.'

'That's easy, then,' she said.

'And bring Archie with you,' he said casually.

'Really? Would that be OK with your landlord? Because you could always have your barbecue here if it would be easier.'

'Unless Archie is going to dig a massive hole in the lawn or chew a chair leg, my landlord will be fine about him visiting,' he said.

She grinned. 'Then I'll bring a tennis ball and a chew with us. He'll be on his best behaviour—and so will I.'

'Good.'

'I really appreciate what you've done for me tonight,' she said. 'You've made a horrible day so much better.'

'You're my girlfriend,' he said softly. 'Of course I'll be there to support you.'

Maybe she'd actually found Mr Right this time, Toni thought. Someone who made her pulse beat faster but who wouldn't make her miserable.

He didn't stay that night, but they managed to sneak in another date during the week—a comedy show in a tiny theatre in Norwich where they held hands through the whole show and just laughed for a couple of hours, forgetting their worries, and then back at Toni's house they sat outside to watch the stars with Archie sprawled at their feet.

'So you like museums if they're about science,' she said.

'Clocks, space and rocks make my nerdy heart happy,' he said. 'I particularly like the display in the Natural History Museum where there's a massive fulgurite.'

'Which is, in English?' she asked.

'Lightning that has struck the earth through sand and turned it to glass—I guess it's a kind of fossilised lightning,' he said.

'Fossilised lightning? Wow. The best I can offer there is to take you back to the stripy cliffs at Hunstanton to find fossils,' she said. 'Or West Runton, where they found a mammoth in the cliff.'

'You are so on.' He smiled at her. 'So what kind of museums do you like?'

'Textiles,' she said promptly. 'I love the

V&A. All the pretty dresses. It's my favourite place in London, and Stacey and I sometimes snatch a day there together.'

'I should have guessed, given how perfect you looked on the nineteen-forties weekend.'

She could tell by his expression that the compliment was genuine, and it warmed her from the inside out. 'Thank you.' She paused. 'What about nature reserves, that kind of thing?'

'The nearest I've been to that in London is walking in one of the parks or alongside the Regent Canal,' he admitted.

'In that case,' she said, 'I know exactly where we're going at the weekend.' She refused to be drawn on the subject until they'd arrived and she'd actually parked the car— this time without Archie accompanying them.

'A seal trip?' he said, seeing the board in the car park.

'This is one of the best bits of Norfolk,' she said. 'It's the biggest colony of grey seals in England—and at this time of year we might be lucky enough to see some common seal pups.'

'That's amazing—I've never actually seen seals that close before,' Ben said when they were on the boat, his eyes wide with wonder. 'They're gorgeous. They remind me of Archie, with those big eyes—except his are amber rather than dark brown.'

'And he's not *quite* as big as the grey seals,' she said with a grin. 'An adult male could be ten times his weight.'

'Remind me of that, next time he plonks himself on my lap,' Ben teased.

He was really relaxed with her dog now, Toni thought. Which was good, because that could've been a real sticking point.

But part of her still worried. Her relationships had all collapsed before. What was to say that this one would last? Would she find herself falling in love with Ben, and then he disappeared, like her exes? The fear brought an edge to her delight in their burgeoning relationship, but she couldn't find the right words to talk about it with him, not without sounding pathetic.

He was right to have insisted on taking a step back from the night when he'd comforted her and stayed. Taking things slowly was a good move. And she could maybe keep a tiny bit of distance between them, protect her heart until they were sure where this was going. Neither of them wanted to face the heartbreak from their past again; and if things went wrong it could make life seriously awkward at work. Even though they were both professional and would always put the needs of the patients first, team meetings would definitely be a source of tension.

So when he kissed her goodbye on her doorstep that night, even though part of her was tempted to ask him to stay, she let him go.

Time. They just needed a little time.

The following week flew by; and early on Friday evening Ben opened his front door to his sister, brother-in-law, niece and nephew.

'The sea air definitely agrees with you, Ben,' Jessie said, hugging him. 'You look happier than I've seen you in years.'

He was—and it was all thanks to Toni. She'd helped him to see the bright side of life again. 'Yeah, yeah,' he said. But he was smiling. 'I'm being lazy and not cooking tonight; I thought we could eat fish and chips on the harbour wall, and then go for a walk by the sea.'

'After the squash on the tube this week in London,' Kit said, 'and the traffic on the M25, that sounds amazing.'

'Bring your stuff in, and we'll go. You must be starving,' Ben said. He showed them to their rooms, then took them down to the harbour. He ended up introducing his family to a dozen or so people while they ate their chips.

'You've really settled in,' Jessie said approvingly.

'It's pretty good here,' Ben said. 'I really like my team. We're having a pot-luck dinner at the head of the practice's house next weekend.'

'That sounds like fun. Maybe I should suggest doing something like that with my team at the lab,' she said thoughtfully.

Jessie, Kit and Kelly all loved the beach; Josh fell asleep in the baby carrier Kit was wearing.

'Can I come and stay in the summer, Uncle Ben, and can we make a huge sandcastle?' Kelly asked.

'And collect shells,' Ben said. 'We can do that tomorrow morning, too, if you like.'

'Yay!' She hugged him. 'I love you, Uncle Ben. You're the best uncle in the world.'

'I love you, too. And you're the best niece in the world,' he said. It made Ben feel a pang of guilt that he'd abandoned his niece, too, by letting his own misery get in the way. He needed to make it up to her.

'I wish you still lived near us in London,' Kelly said wistfully.

'I've missed you, too, Kelly,' he said, and hauled her up to sit on his shoulders. 'But you can all come and see me any time you like. Plus I can still read you a bedtime story over a video call. We'll make it a regular thing. Every Monday evening.'

'I love you,' she said again.

'You're going to meet a very special dog tomorrow. One of the people I work with has a therapy dog who loves reading time, and he'd like to meet you.'

'Would this dog happen to belong to the nurse practitioner?' Jessie asked, her tone deceptively mild.

'My colleague Toni, yes,' Ben said, trying to keep his voice casual.

'Hmm,' Jessie said. 'Colleague.'

He sighed. 'All right. She's my girlfriend, too, but we're taking things steady and getting to know each other.'

'I'm glad you've moved on,' she said.

'I'm in the process of doing that,' he said softly. 'There's still a bit of me that's scared it could all go wrong. And she's been hurt in the past, too.'

'Maybe you'll be good for each other.'

'Maybe.' It was so hard to trust again. To let himself relax and take the risk of falling for Toni. To believe that this time it wouldn't go wrong.

On Saturday morning, Ben took everyone to the beach again. They made a massive sandcastle, to Kelly's delight, and collected a pocketful of really pretty shells.

'I'm going to make a magic mirror,' Kelly said, 'and stick the shells around the edge.'

'Great idea, Kelly,' he said with a smile.

'And I'm going to wish—no, I can't tell you that, or it won't come true.'

Ben knew what he wished for. But, like his niece, he wasn't going to tell anyone, because he really wanted it to come true. For him and Toni to be together and have a happy-ever-after. For it to work out this time. For him to be *enough* for Toni, the way he hadn't been for Karen.

Meeting Ben's sister. Part of Toni was panicking about it. Supposing Ben's family didn't like her? Then again, Sean's family had loved her, and look how badly that had turned out. All she could do was be herself. And she really ought to tell Stacey that she and Ben were more than just friends—though, given the indulgent smile on her sister's face, Toni had a feeling that Stacey already knew.

She clipped Archie's harness into the seatbelt, then drove over to Ben's house.

When he opened the door to her, his smile warmed her all the way through.

'Thanks for coming,' he said, and stole a kiss. 'Come and meet everyone.'

'Okay.'

'Toni, this is my sister Jessie, my brother-in-law Kit, my niece Kelly and my nephew Josh,' he said, shepherding her through to the kitchen where his sister was chopping a salad.

'Lovely to meet you,' Toni said with a smile.

'Everyone, this is Toni, and her dog, Archie,' Ben said.

'Lovely to meet you, too,' Jessie said.

'I've brought pudding,' Toni said. 'Vanilla cheesecake—home-made—and strawberries that I picked from my garden just before I left.' She handed Ben two plastic boxes and a bottle of wine.

'I love cheesecake,' Jessie said.

'I love strawberries,' Kelly added shyly.

Josh simply cooed from his father's arms and pointed at the dog.

'Would you like to come and play with Archie in the garden, Kelly?' Toni asked. 'He's been looking forward to meeting you.'

Kelly looked at her mother.

'We'll both come and we'll leave the men to finish making the salad,' Jessie said.

Meaning Jessie would be able to ask questions without making it awkward for Ben, Toni thought.

'OK,' Ben said. He stroked Archie's head. 'And, yes, I'll make sure we save a sausage for you.'

Archie gave a soft woof of appreciation.

'That's something I'd never thought I'd see,' Jessie said. 'Ben isn't a dog person.'

'He's kind of got used to Archie being around,' Toni said. 'Sit, Archie, and give Kelly a high five.'

To the little girl's obvious delight, the dog sat nicely and lifted his paw.

'That's so cool!' Kelly said, looking thrilled.

'Ben said he's a therapy dog. How does that work?' Jessie asked.

'We do a session once a week at the nursing home, where basically he sits and lets them make a fuss of him and talk to him. Having him around is brilliant for the residents, because having a canine visitor gives them something to focus on apart from their illness. Plus studies show that making a fuss of a dog brings down people's blood pressure, so it's good for them physically as well as mentally,' Toni said. 'The team at our nursing home say that Archie helps with more than just the residents' moods; they tend to interact more with each other and the staff after they've seen him. So he's really good for them. And he enjoys his work.'

'That sounds lovely,' Jessie said.

'It's nice to give something back—it's the nursing home where my grandmother was when her dementia meant she needed more care than my sister and I could give her. Her best friend Ginny, who was kind of like a second grandmother to me and my sister when we were growing up, ended up being cared for there, too. And once a week we go to the local infant school and the reluctant readers read to Archie. I know that sounds a bit airy-fairy,' Toni said with a smile, 'but it's brought their reading age on by an average of three months in the last term. They stop worrying so much when they read to him, and it helps them focus.'

'That,' Jessie said, 'is amazing.'

'It's lovely to be able to make such a difference. And Archie loves it, too. He's a very sociable dog.' Toni paused. 'Ben told me you're a research chemist.'

Jessie nodded. 'I'm a biochemist. I've just gone back after maternity leave and I'm working on a new cancer drug at the moment.'

'That's wonderful,' Toni said.

'I'm so glad Ben's settled in. He keeps telling me he's fine, but I've been worrying about him,' Jessie said. 'Seeing him for myself has made me feel a lot better. He looks a lot more relaxed.'

'He's a good man, and everyone in the village has responded to that,' Toni said. 'And I think this place is good for him, too.'

'Did he tell you about…?' Jessie bit her lip, looking awkward.

Toni guessed what Jessie meant. The thing that had driven Ben away from London. 'His ex falling for his best friend and them having a baby while she was still married to Ben, yes. That was pretty rough on him.'

'It pretty much broke his he—' Jessie stopped and gave an over-bright smile. 'Hey, Ben.'

'As it's warm out here, I thought you might like a drink,' he said, nodding at the tray he was carrying, which contained a pitcher of home-made lemonade and glasses.

Jessie blushed. 'Thank you. Sorry. I wasn't gossiping.'

'You're my little sister and you worry about me, I know. But I'm fine. I'm moving on,' he said gently, and ruffled her hair.

Jessie didn't bring up the subject after Ben had gone back to the kitchen, so they chatted while Kelly threw the tennis ball for Archie, who brought it back, dropped it at her feet and wagged his tail hopefully at her until she did it all over again.

By the time that Ben and Kit emerged from the kitchen together, ready to start the barbecue, Jessie and Toni had become firm friends.

Once the food was ready, they ate out in the garden, with Archie waiting patiently for his share of sausages and chicken to cool. And baby Josh—who'd woken briefly to eat puréed chicken casserole and mashed banana—was asleep in his pram.

'You're so lucky, living by the sea,' Jessie said. 'Have you always lived here, Toni?'

'Since I was twelve—my grandmother brought my sister Stacey and me to live with her after our mum and dad were killed in a car crash,' Toni said. 'I trained in London and worked in the emergency department at the London Victoria, but I moved back here when Gran became ill and needed support. But it's a wonderful village.' She smiled. 'And Ben has the entire village falling at his feet since the nineteen-forties weekend. Half of them were bowled over by his baking and the other half by his dancing.'

'I wish I'd known about it,' Jessie said. 'It sounds like a lot of fun.'

'It is. Come next year,' Toni suggested. 'Ben told me he went to dance lessons with you. Maybe you can do a demo of the jitterbug for us at the village hall.' She gave Jessie a sidelong look. 'You could always give me a demo now...'

Jessie laughed. 'I'm a bit out of practice.'

'Go on, love. You're fabulous,' Kit said.

'Please, Mummy? Please, Uncle Ben?' Kelly asked. 'And I can dance with Daddy.'

'What about Toni?' Jessie asked.

'Don't ask me to dance. I have two left feet. Archie and I can give you marks—just like in *Strictly Come Dancing*,' Toni said with a grin. 'I think you should earn your cheesecake, Jessie.'

Ben found some music on his phone, and the four of them danced a very energetic jitterbug. Toni clapped when they had finished. 'I award both couples a perfect ten,' she said. 'What about you, Archie?'

The dog barked softly twice.

'That's Archie-speak for "me, too",' Toni said.

'But you're not getting away without dancing,' Ben said, and took her hand.

'Me and Archie will be the judges now,' Kelly said.

So what could she do but join in? Ben led her round the garden and, just like the first time she'd danced with him, she felt as if she was dancing on air. Everything melted away, as if it was just the two of them, while the sun began to set.

For a moment, she thought he was going to kiss her. His sea-green eyes were dark and deep with emotion. But then the music ended and Kelly started clapping, breaking the spell, and Josh woke up and began crying.

Kit lifted the baby out of the pram. 'Bath and a change for you, young man, and then some milk.'

Toni was thrilled when Jessie asked her if she'd like to feed the baby. 'I love babies,' she said. 'I have a fourteen-month-old niece. It's been fabulous seeing her grow and change.'

Ben looked at the two parts of his life colliding. Seeing Toni cuddling his nephew felt odd. And then he realised why: he didn't feel as if he had to insulate his heart any more. Seeing his girlfriend holding a baby didn't remind him of what he'd lost; instead, it gave him hope that he was finally moving on.

After Toni had fed the baby and handed him back to his mum, she ended up reading a story to Kelly, with the little girl sitting on her lap and Archie's head on both their knees. When the little girl's eyelids started to droop and the spaniel's eyes were closed, she said gently, 'I think I need to take Archie home to bed now, Kelly. He's really tired. But we've had a lovely time with you all today and we're both very glad we met you.'

'Can you come back tomorrow? Uncle Ben is taking us on a steam train,' Kelly said.

Toni smiled. 'Thank you for asking me, and although I'd love to join you I'm afraid I can't because I'm seeing my sister tomorrow.'

'She can come, too,' Kelly said.

Toni ruffled her hair. 'Another time. That's a definite date.'

Once she'd said her goodbyes, Ben saw her to the door. 'Thank you for coming today.'

'I've had a wonderful time. I like your family very much.'

'It's entirely mutual.' He kissed her. 'I'll call you later.'

'OK.' She snatched a last kiss. 'Have fun at the steam train tomorrow.'

Jessie waited until Kit was putting Kelly to bed before tackling Ben. 'She's lovely. And so is that beautiful dog.'

'He's a therapy dog. He's trained to be like that.'

'I liked Toni a lot. She's kind, she's sweet and she's great with Kelly. I know it's early days,' Jessie continued. 'But I saw the way you look at each other. And Kelly was going to say a last goodbye to Toni and Archie, but she said you were kissing Toni so she thought she'd better come back.'

'I didn't even hear Kelly coming into the hallway,' Ben admitted.

'You've got it bad,' Jessie said with a smile. 'I gather you've told her about Karen and the baby?'

He nodded.

'I'm glad. I liked her a lot. She was telling me about the therapy dog work. That's such a lovely thing to do. She's definitely one of the good guys.'

'And she's been hurt before,' he said. 'By someone who sounds as if he was incredibly selfish. So we're taking things slowly.' He and Toni hadn't exactly taken things slowly so far, he thought, trying to hold back the colour that threatened to rush into his face. But they were dating properly now. Getting to know each other. Seeing where this thing took them—and if he could finally let go and learn to trust again.

'I think,' Jessie said, 'you might be just what each other needs.'

And he had a feeling his sister was right.

CHAPTER NINE

'YOU MADE A real hit with my sister,' Ben told Toni on Monday evening, when they'd taken Archie for a long walk on the beach.

'I liked her very much, too,' Toni said. 'Kit seemed lovely—and Kelly and Josh are adorable.'

'So,' Ben said, 'are you.'

Which thrilled her to her bones, and they walked back down to the harbour with their arms wrapped around each other.

On Thursday, it was Ginny's funeral; although it was good to share memories with Ginny's family and friends, it also made Toni really miss her grandmother and her parents, and by the time she got home she felt really flat and miserable. Even a cuddle with Archie wasn't enough to fill the empty spaces.

That evening Ben brought dinner round to Toni's—for Stacey, Nick and Scarlett, too.

Stacey gave him a hug. 'I know I'm not supposed to know anything about what's going on between you two, but I'm glad you and Toni have found each other.'

'Me, too,' Ben said softly.

On Saturday it was the practice's pot-luck dinner. Ranjit had a trestle table set up for the food and plenty of chairs; although Toni and Ben arrived separately, they managed to sit together in the garden.

Ben had brought lemon-glazed chicken and sweet potato wedges; and Toni had made a lemon tart with an almond pastry base, supplementing it with fruit from her garden. By the time everyone from the practice arrived, the table was groaning.

After dinner, Toni instigated a round of charades that had everyone enjoying themselves, from the younger children through to the teenagers as well as the entire practice team. When Ranjit put some music on, Ben ended up giving everyone an impromptu dance lesson. And at the end of the evening Ben insisted on walking Toni home.

'I really enjoyed tonight,' he said. 'Our team is lovely, and so are their families.'

'Plus we've got loads of recipes now for our patients. I'll need to run them all through one of the nutrition sites so I can work out the calories, fat, carbohydrate and protein content,' she said, 'but I think we've got a really good base for our meal plans now.'

'I'll send you the photographs I took of all the dishes,' Ben said.

'Thanks. A picture might be the thing that persuades someone to try making a dish,' she said.

At her doorstep, she asked, 'Would you like to come in?'

'Very much,' he said. 'I want to dance with you again.'

'You sort out the music, and I'll pour the wine.'

Swaying with her to a soft bluesy track, with their arms wrapped round each other, made Ben feel at peace with the world. And it was a wrench saying goodnight to her. He was oh, so close to asking her if he could stay. But he knew that rushing things wasn't the way forward. He still needed time to learn to trust. To put the past behind him. To be sure that he could give his heart again.

On Wednesday, Toni's eyes were sparkling when they took Archie for a run on the beach. 'Stacey texted me earlier to see if you're free on Sunday. She and Nick are hiring a boat on the Broads. Would you like to come with us?'

'The Norfolk Broads, as in the Bowie song?' he asked.

She smiled. 'Absolutely. They're actually medieval peat diggings which filled up over the years to make a series of lakes and channels. The scenery is amazing, and so is the wildlife. I know you enjoyed the seals, so I thought you might enjoy this, too.'

'So is this an official date with your family?' Like the barbecue had been with his sister.

'If you want it to be,' she said.

He thought about it. This would be the next step. And when he was with her like this, just the two of them and her dog, he felt so light of spirit. Would it change things if they went public? Would *she* change?

He decided to take the risk. 'Official. OK. That's good with me.'

'We're leaving at about ten. We're taking sandwiches for lunch and stopping for dinner at a pub on the way home, if that's all right with you.'

'That's great.'

She smiled. 'Then I'll pick you up at ten minutes to ten.'

'I'll be ready,' he promised.

On Sunday, when she picked him up, Ben wasn't that surprised when he discovered that Archie was coming, too; but he was surprised to discover that the dog had a lifejacket.

'I had no idea they made lifejackets for dogs,' he said.

'The same as for small children,' Stacey told him with a smile, and he saw that Scarlett, too, had a special lifejacket.

Nick and Ben took turns steering the boat while Toni and Stacey took turns cuddling Scarlett and pointing out all the wildlife to her—coots and moorhens on the water, along with the ducks, huge swallowtail butterflies in the bushes, and even a bright blue kingfisher swooping down.

Ben watched Toni cuddling her niece, patiently teaching her new words and clapping when she got them right.

She was so good with children. She'd make a brilliant mother.

But he'd thought that about Karen, and look where that had got him.

He pulled himself up sharply. It was time he put the past to rest. To draw a line, put it behind him and focus on the good—on his new life here, in a little seaside village full of people who were prepared to open their hearts to him, instead of brooding.

'You're quiet,' Toni said, coming to join him at the front of the boat while Nick went to see his wife and daughter.

'I'm fine,' he fibbed.

'Are you feeling a bit seasick or anything?'

'No.' He didn't want to tell her how ridiculous and self-indulgent he was being. He wanted her to enjoy the day. 'Show me what you were showing Scarlett. I'm a city boy at heart so I know absolutely nothing about flora and fauna.'

To his relief she didn't push him. Instead she did what he'd asked. 'OK. See all those water grasses at the edge of the Broads? Sedges have edges, and reeds are round. The reeds are the ones that are harvested and dried to make roofs for the thatched cottages around here.'

'Right.'

'And those black birds swimming over there are moorhens and coots.'

'What's the difference?' He frowned. 'I've heard the saying "bald as a coot", but they don't actually look bald.'

She laughed. 'No, they're not. I've no idea where that saying comes from.'

'Maybe it's the same as "bald eagle",' he said, 'so it's to do with having white feathers?'

'Maybe,' she said. 'The coots have the white bills and the moorhens have the red bills. The way to remember which one is "moorhen, more colour".'

Ben thoroughly enjoyed the journey, seeing the windmills and the waterways and the stunning range of flora and fauna. But even more he enjoyed being close to Toni and her family.

That night, when she dropped him home, he waited a moment before opening the car door. 'Are you doing anything next weekend?'

'I don't think there's anything in my diary. Why?' she asked.

'I was thinking, it might be nice to go away for the weekend. If you can get time off on Friday afternoon, maybe we could have a weekend away.'

'A romantic mini-break? That sounds wonderful.'

'Abroad, maybe. Except, even if you have a pet passport, I'm not sure that it'd be fair to take Archie on a city break.'

She looked thoughtful. 'It's the school summer holidays now, so I probably can't get him into the boarding kennels at this short notice, but I'm pretty sure Stacey will have him to stay. Though I'd rather check with her first before you book anywhere.'

'Sure,' he said. 'Let me know, and then I'll book somewhere. Can I surprise you?'

'That,' she said, 'would be lovely.'

Stacey was happy to look after Archie for the weekend, so Ben booked a weekend away, refusing to tell Toni anything more than what the temperature was likely to be and what she'd need to pack. He managed to keep the surprise of where they were going until they checked in at the airport and it was obvious from the check-in desk.

'Vienna? How lovely,' she said. 'I've never been there before.'

'I believe it's all about cake, chandeliers

and coffee,' he said with a smile. 'I thought we could just wander round the city, visit art galleries and gardens and old palaces, and have plenty of stops for coffee and cake.'

'That sounds perfect—really romantic,' she said.

And it was. The hotel was gorgeous, converted from an old palace, with high ceilings, chandeliers and marble floors, and a view from their window over the park.

'I thought we could maybe start with the Sisi Museum in the Imperial Apartments,' Ben said. 'I think there's an exhibition of Empress Elisabeth's clothes.'

Toni was thrilled that he'd remembered her love of costume museums. 'That sounds fabulous, but won't you be a bit bored?'

He smiled back. 'Not with you.'

Toni was enthralled by the displays and the paintings. 'This replica of Sisi's wedding dress is incredible. And that gown in the painting with the stars in her hair—that's stunning.'

'So would you dress up in something like that?' he asked, intrigued.

'Maybe.' She smiled at him. 'I can imagine you dressed up as a nineteenth-century aristocrat, in a tail coat and a white cravat.' Mischief danced in her eyes. 'And a top hat.'

He grinned. 'A top hat to me means Fred Astaire.'

'But I'm no Ginger Rogers,' she said. 'If I tap dance with you, your toes would be sulking for the next decade.'

He laughed and stole a kiss. 'Don't be so hard on yourself.'

Though Ben was hard on himself, she thought. He blamed himself for his wife's betrayal, thinking he hadn't been enough for her. And that wasn't fair. Here in Vienna, would the magic of the city work on him, the way it was working on her?

Toni had brought a little black dress with her and they ate at the hotel's Michelin-starred restaurant that night before strolling through the city centre with their arms wrapped round each other, charmed by the string quartets and opera singers on every corner.

'This is such a treat,' she said. 'Fabulous food, beautiful architecture, those gorgeous dresses in the museum and this wonderful music. I don't think I've ever heard buskers as amazing as this before.'

'Me, too. And you're the perfect person

to share it with.' He smiled. 'And now we're going to have a twilight tour of the city.'

He helped her up into a *fiaker*, one of the horse-drawn carriages that lined up near the cathedral, and sat with his arm round her as they drove through the cobbled streets. The carriage driver pointed out places of interest as he drove them round the city. Places where Mozart and Beethoven and Haydn had lived, the Parliament building, the Hofburg Palace and the Opera House.

'Imagine being here nearly two hundred years ago,' she said, her expression wistful, 'and driving in one of these carriages to the theatre, then hearing Beethoven's Ninth played for the very first time...'

'Funny you should say that,' he said. 'We have tickets for a concert tomorrow night. It's not Beethoven's Ninth, but something I hope is special.'

She smiled at him. 'I'm with you. Of course it'll be special.'

And the ice that had surrounded his heart for the last few months finally cracked. Right here, right now, Ben thought, he couldn't be any happier. The empty spaces inside him began to feel full of light. Vienna was called the city of dreams as well as the city of music. Would his dreams of the future finally start to come true with Toni?

That night, Ben waltzed barefoot with Toni in their suite, before undressing her slowly, carrying her over to the bed and making slow, sweet love with her. It was the first time they had made love since that night when she'd been so desperate for comfort; but this time was all the sweeter because it was just for them. No past, no sorrow to get in the way—just the sheer joy of being together.

And there was no awkwardness the next morning when she woke, warm and comfortable in his arms: just closeness and sweetness and looking forward to the rest of the weekend.

'So is it the first time you've been to Vienna?' she asked over a breakfast of good coffee, freshly squeezed orange juice and amazing pastries.

'Yes. You?'

She smiled. 'Yes. And I'm so glad we're going to explore it together.'

'I thought we could do the art galleries today—and have a wander through the gardens, as it's so sunny outside,' he said.

'That sounds perfect.'

And it was: Toni thoroughly enjoyed walking hand in hand with Ben in the public gardens, discovering that they liked the same kind of art, and taking selfies with the fountains of the Belvedere Gardens behind them, and the massive white palace with its green copper roof reflected in the lake.

They stopped at one of the oldest cafés in the city for coffee and cake.

'Vienna is famous for the Sachertorte,' Ben said. 'We really ought to try it.'

'Is there a non-chocolate version?' she asked hopefully.

'That's the whole point of it. Chocolate overload, and it's meant to be amazing— even you might like it.'

'How about a compromise?' she suggested. 'I try a forkful of yours, and you try whatever I choose.'

'Deal,' he said with a smile.

It took her ages to choose a cake from the huge selection in the glass-fronted cabinet, but eventually she chose Esterhazy torte, a stripy layered confection of almond meringue and buttercream.

The melange coffee, the Viennese version of a cappuccino, was perfect—but the cake wasn't. 'Sorry. It's much too rich for me. I know I'm a heathen,' she said ruefully.

But she enjoyed feeding Ben a forkful of her own cake, watching his sea-green eyes widening in bliss. Seeing the curve of his mouth and remembering how it felt against hers.

'That's sublime,' he said. 'Though I have to admit I prefer mine.'

'Stacey would agree with you,' she said.

'They sell smaller versions of the big *tortes* in the shop, here,' he said. 'Maybe we can take one back for her.'

'Great idea.' She smiled at him. 'I'm so glad we came here, Ben.'

The day got even better, with a wander round the Gothic cathedral with its mosaic tiled roof where Mozart had got married, a stroll through the streets, and then a quick traditional dinner of schnitzel with potato salad.

'I really hope you like this,' Ben said as they reached the tiny concert hall.

'This is amazing,' Toni whispered as they took their seats. The room was gorgeously baroque, from the ornate floral decoration on the walls through to the stunning Venetian glass chandelier. Better still, the musicians were all wearing period dress. She could just imagine being here two hundred years ago, as she'd said to him the previous night in the *fiaker*.

'This is where Mozart himself played to selected audiences,' Ben told her, and he held her hand throughout the performance, his fingers warm and sure around hers.

Toni recognised the music as some of Mozart's most famous: *Eine Kleine Nacht-musik*, along with the *Dissonance* quartet that he'd dedicated to Haydn. The musicians were superb and it would've been a treat in any concert hall, but here it was even better. And she really, really loved the costumes. She couldn't have imagined a more perfect evening.

'That was so special. Thank you,' she said when the concert was over.

What was even more special was sharing the sheer joy of the music with Ben.

As they wandered back to the hotel, their arms wrapped around each other, Toni was pretty sure she was falling in love with Ben. With this thoughtful, gentle man who also never hesitated to do the right thing, the man who had pushed himself to overcome his wariness of dogs to make friends with

Archie, and who made her world feel like a better place.

Not that she was going to spook him by telling him. Not yet. She knew he still needed time to get over the collapse of his marriage; but she hoped that spending time with her and her family was helping him to do that.

It was raining the next morning, but the weather couldn't spoil their mood. 'Perhaps we should do something indoors this morning,' Ben said. 'How about the rest of the Imperial Apartments and the butterfly house?'

'Sounds perfect,' Toni said.

She enjoyed wandering around the Imperial Apartments; and then they headed for the butterfly house. The tropical interior with its waterfall, pond, bridges and palm trees was gorgeous; and there were hundreds of butterflies flying freely, of all colours and sizes—from blues to bright orange, vivid red to yellow. Toni was fascinated by the huge owl butterflies with their enormous spots like an owl's eye in the middle of their wings, resting and feeding from a peach on one of the tables.

'This feels magical,' she said. 'I've never been anywhere like this before.'

'It's amazing,' he agreed. 'And I'm so glad I'm here with you.'

His smile made her feel as if the weather outside was bright sunshine rather than pouring rain. They'd become closer over the last couple of days, more in tune with each other, and Toni was convinced that Ben really was the one for her. That she could trust him with her heart, and know he'd be there for her— just as she would be there for him.

Finally they travelled back to England and went to pick up Archie from Toni's sister.

'We brought cake to say thank you for looking after Archie,' Toni told Stacey, handing her a beautifully wrapped package.

'I recognise the name on the packaging. This isn't just cake,' Stacey said, her eyes widening. 'It's the best chocolate cake in the world.'

'I did try a forkful of Ben's,' Toni said, 'but I much preferred the Esterhazy torte, all almond and buttercream.'

Ben laughed. 'I'm with you, Stacey. Every cake I tried in Vienna was chocolate-based, but this one was definitely the best.'

'Thank you.' Stacey hugged them both.

'We brought you some chocolate as well,' Ben said. 'The little ones shaped like kittens are for Scarlett. And there's some proper Viennese coffee.'

'You really didn't have to spoil us quite so much,' Stacey said. 'We've loved having Archie for the weekend. I'm your sister, Toni, and I know you'd do exactly the same for me if it was the other way round.'

'We just wanted to bring you something nice,' Toni said. 'And we saw butterflies.'

'Look, Scarlett.' Ben showed the toddler his picture of the owl butterfly that had landed on his hand.

'Oooh!' Scarlett said, beaming and pointing at the butterfly.

'Maybe we can go and see some butterflies together,' Ben said. 'As a family.'

Toni glanced at her sister, and was gratified to see the warmth of her smile. And she knew exactly what her sister was thinking: *This time, you've found Mr Right.*

Life didn't get any better than this, Ben thought. He hadn't been this happy in years. He loved his job, he loved his morning run on the beach—and he was definitely falling in love with the nurse practitioner and her dog.

But in the middle of the week, he and Toni were watching the sunset from her garden when her phone beeped to signal an incoming text.

She glanced at the screen. 'Nothing important. It can wait,' she said.

But Ben had glanced at the screen at the same time, more out of habit than nosiness. The problem was that he'd seen the message—and he'd seen who it was from.

Sean. Her ex. Why was he texting her, and especially with that kind of message? It was a couple of years since they'd broken up, and Ben knew that Toni had been hurt by the split. She certainly hadn't mentioned staying in touch with her ex.

Though he could hardly demand to know why Sean was texting her, or why she even still had his number on her phone, because that reeked of paranoia. He knew Toni wasn't like Karen; but, despite that, he couldn't stop that tiny little seed of doubt creeping into his mind. Was he making the same mistake all over again? Was he trying so hard to convince himself that the future was bright that he was missing something?

Of course not. He was being utterly ridiculous.

But the thought wouldn't go away, and he ended up making a feeble excuse and going back to his own home instead of staying at Toni's that night.

Had something happened? Toni wondered. Ben had been really quiet that evening.

Or maybe he was just tired.

She made herself a cup of tea, and turned her attention to the text she'd ignored earlier.

Can you call me? I miss you.

She rolled her eyes, not believing a word of it. It was more likely that either Sean had sent it to her by accident, or he had some kind of event coming up where he needed to schmooze for the sake of his career, and he'd just split up with someone and wanted a reliable plus one to step into the breach.

She could ignore it, but that might mean he'd take her silence as meaning that he needed to make some kind of charm offensive. She really wasn't interested.

Quickly, she typed a reply.

Assume you sent that text to me in error. Toni.

He didn't text her again, so she assumed her guess to be right. Obviously Sean, being Sean, couldn't be bothered even to acknowledge her texts—because then he would have to acknowledge he'd made an error, and Sean could do no wrong in his own eyes.

She'd had such a lucky escape. She was so grateful that Ben wasn't like that. He had at least opened up to her and talked. He listened to her. And, after Vienna, she felt that he was the one she could commit to—and he would be just as committed to her.

Over the next few days, life felt just about perfect for Toni. She was really in tune with Ben, both at work and outside it. They'd worked on the new practice website pages between them and had received a lot of compliments from their patients, as well as more suggestions of recipes to tweak. And she was very close to the point where she was ready to go public to everyone, not just their families, with the fact that she and Ben were a couple. There were some moments when she felt as if he was holding something back, but she thought she was probably just being paranoid and stupid.

And then on Wednesday morning she woke up feeling odd.

Her breasts were sore and she felt a bit queasy. And one mouthful of coffee for breakfast made her gag.

If any of her patients had come to see her with those symptoms, she would've suggested that they do a pregnancy test...

She shook herself. Of course she wasn't pregnant. She and Ben had taken precautions.

But she knew that the only one hundred per cent form of contraception was abstinence. Considering that she gave a talk every year at the local high school on that particular topic...

She counted back mentally to the date of her last period, and went cold.

It was eight weeks ago.

Surely she'd made a mistake? Maybe there was another reason why her period was late.

Except she couldn't think of one.

Eight weeks. Which meant that conception would've been six weeks ago. Around the time that Ginny had died. She'd been upset, and she and Ben had ended up making love for the first time. Had they taken precautions? She couldn't remember. She couldn't think straight.

The chances were that she wasn't pregnant and this was just a blip in her cycle. But the only way to put her mind properly at rest was to do a pregnancy test.

No way could she buy a test from anywhere in Great Crowmell, because speculation would go round the village like wildfire. She'd have to go somewhere else to buy it, somewhere that nobody knew her.

It was just as well that Ben hadn't stayed here last night, because until she knew one way or the other about this she really couldn't face him.

Term had finished, so she had a free morning instead of taking Archie to the infant school for their reading session. If she drove into Norwich, she'd be able to pick up a pregnancy test, do it, and be back in Great Crowmell before her afternoon shift.

Archie had clearly picked up that something was wrong, because he sat as close to her as he could, as if trying to comfort her.

'It's all going to be fine, Arch,' she reassured him.

It had to be.

She drove to the city, parked, bought the test, and headed for the public toilets in the library building. Thankfully it was too early for it to be busy, so she didn't feel guilty about staying in the cubicle while she waited for the test to finish working.

According to the packaging, she'd have the results within three minutes. She'd bought a digital one so there could be no mistake, no squinting at the little screen to see if there was a faint line.

The hour-glass symbol flashed at her to let her know that the test was working. But the seconds seemed to stretch on and on. How was it that time could fly by while she was at the beach with her dog, yet now it dragged? She kept staring at the screen, willing it to change and willing it to tell her what she needed to know.

Three minutes of limbo.

Three minutes that went on and on and on.

Three minutes of...

Pregnant.

Adrenalin flooded through her, making her hands shake, and she dropped the test stick.

When she picked it up again there was a figure on the line below the words: *3+—*

meaning that it was more than three weeks since conception. Which tied in with what she'd half suspected: she'd become pregnant the day of Ginny's death. When she'd thought she was celebrating life with Ben, they were actually making a new life together.

What now?

What now?

The question echoed like a heartbeat.

Sitting there locked in a public toilet cubicle wasn't going to help. She'd have to face this and think about the possible ways forward.

Carefully, she slid the test back inside the box, then replaced the box in her handbag.

One foot in front of the other.

She washed her hands, then walked down to the cathedral. Maybe here she could get her thoughts together. She went over to the huge openwork metal globe where a couple of candles were already lit, put some money into the offering box and lit a candle for her mother, her father, her grandmother and Ginny. The huge, soaring space of the building helped to still some of the turbulence in her head; she walked quietly over to the door that led to the cloisters, and then out into the green space in the centre where the labyrinth lay.

Walking a labyrinth was a good way to meditate. Putting one foot in front of the other, following the twists and turns of the pattern and knowing it was a continuous path rather than having dead ends to baffle her, helped. And, by the time she reached the centre, her thoughts had settled enough that she knew what she wanted to do.

This baby was hers and Ben's. Toni understood now the bittersweetness that Stacey must have faced during her pregnancy with Scarlett, knowing that their parents and their grandmother weren't there with them physically to cuddle the baby and share their joy. But at the same time she knew she'd see bits of them in her baby, just as she saw them in her niece Scarlett—a smile, an expression, the curve of her face. Little traits that went from generation to generation, love that was passed down through the years. And they'd always be there in her heart.

One thing was for definite: although this baby wasn't planned, it was wanted. She was going to keep it.

And she wanted to share the baby with Ben. He was the kind of man she knew she could trust, who would be there to support her dreams, and he would always be there in the tough times. More than that, he made her heart beat faster, made her feel as if the sun was shining even on a drizzly day. He was nothing like the selfish egotists she'd dated in the past.

But how would he feel about an unplanned pregnancy?

He'd been here before, and it had all gone horribly wrong.

This time round, the situation was a little different. He knew she wasn't seeing anyone else, and he'd know for sure that he was the father. But this pregnancy was still going to bring back bad memories for him—memories of rejection and loss.

She had absolutely no idea how he'd react. She knew he'd wanted to make a family; he'd told her that he'd been broody and looked forward to being a father. Had that changed, because of Karen's affair? Would he see this as a second chance, a way for everything to be right, this time round? Or would it totally mess with his head? Would it heal the hurt, or make it worse?

She'd have to find the right words to tell him.

What if he didn't want to make a family with her?

Toni dragged in a breath. Stacey and Nick would be there for her, she knew, and she was sure that Jessie would want to be involved in the life of her niece or nephew.

But Ben…

It was the one area where she wasn't quite sure of him. He'd want to do the right thing, she was sure—but the personal cost might be too high. She didn't want to hurt him, but she was scared that this might be the point where it would all go wrong between them.

She sat in the cathedral grounds for a while longer, taking strength from its peace and serenity. And then she drove back to Great Crowmell in time for her afternoon shift. Though before she saw her first patient she texted Ben.

Can you meet me outside Scott's after work, please? We need to talk.

CHAPTER TEN

Can you meet me outside Scott's after work, please? We need to talk.

BEN STARED AT the message Toni had sent him.

He had the strongest feeling that something was wrong, but he had no idea what. Clearly it was something big enough for her to want to talk about it face to face.

Yes, sure, he texted back.

He'd thought that things were going well between them, that they'd grown closer since their weekend in Vienna, but had he been deluding himself? Had she changed her mind? Even though he tried to ignore it, the thought went through his mind: was it anything to do with the text she'd received from Sean and never mentioned? Was he making a fool of himself all over again?

He focused on his patients for the rest of the afternoon, putting his worries in the back of his head, but the worries all rushed back when he arrived in the car park outside Scott's Café and Toni was sitting on one of the benches without Archie.

She never came to the beach without her dog.

Had something happened to the dog? No, surely not. She wouldn't have said they needed to talk. She would've told him if Archie was ill or hurt—or worse.

'Hi. Where's Archie?' he asked.

'At home. I came straight here from work.'

So whatever the problem was, he was pretty sure now that it was about them.

'Want to walk?' he asked.

She nodded, and they headed out to the dunes—but she didn't hold his hand, the way she had done for the last couple of weeks or so. And he had a nasty feeling that if he tried to hold her hand right now, she'd pull away. It was as if there was some kind of invisible force-field round her, keeping him at a distance. She didn't talk, either. This really, really wasn't like her.

When they got to the dunes, he stopped

and looked her in the eye. 'What's wrong, Toni?'

Her beautiful grey eyes were filled with anguish, and she took a deep breath. 'There isn't an easy way to say this.'

She wanted to call a halt to their relationship? So he'd been right to be paranoid, and that text from her ex really had been the beginning of the end. It felt as if he'd been sucker-punched, but he wasn't a coward. 'Tell me straight, then,' he said, trying to keep his voice as neutral as possible so he didn't put any pressure on her.

He was expecting to hear the words 'I can't do this any more,' or 'it's not working'; what she said instead shocked him so much that he couldn't quite take it in. Had she *really* just told him that, or had he misheard?

'What did you just say?' he asked, needing her to repeat it so it would sink in properly.

'I'm pregnant,' she said.

It felt as if all the air had been sucked out of his lungs.

He'd been here before and it had ended so badly. He knew Toni hadn't been dating someone else secretly, but he could still remember seeing the anguish on Karen's face and hearing the words tumble out, the horrible truth. A little voice in his head whispered, *Here we go all over again. How do you know you can trust her? How do you know that text was innocent when she's never talked to you about it?*

He shoved the thoughts away and tried to focus on the facts.

Toni was pregnant.

With his baby.

How could it have happened, when they'd taken precautions?

Well, of course he knew the science of it. He was a GP. He knew that there was always a tiny chance that contraception would fail, even if you were careful. The only one hundred per cent guaranteed form of contraception was abstinence.

Right at that moment, he didn't know what to say. What to do. His brain just wasn't functioning. There weren't any words in his head, just white noise: as if it had suddenly become winter and a storm had sent the waves crashing onto the shore.

But he had to say something. He couldn't just stand here in silence, watching her wilt visibly before him.

He opened his mouth, intending to ask her if she was all right, but what came out was, 'I need time to think.'

Toni thought she'd prepared herself mentally for Ben having difficulty with her news, but she really hadn't. That wasn't just shock on his face, it was absolute horror.

He was going to let his past get in the way of his future. What had happened to him was horrible, yes, but she'd never given him any reason to think she would cheat on him. And she really resented the fact that he was treating her as if she'd behaved in the same way as his ex, when she hadn't.

Which meant that she'd managed, yet again, to pick Mr Wrong. He didn't want to make a family with her. She'd fallen for someone who didn't want her. Someone who'd maybe seen her as his transition partner rather than his for ever partner. And who wasn't ready even to talk, let alone have a real relationship. She was going to have to be brave.

She took a deep breath and willed her face and her voice to stay as neutral as possible. She wasn't going to let him know how much this hurt. 'OK. You need time to think. I'll give you that. Call me when you're ready to discuss things.'

And then she turned away before he could see the tears filming in her eyes, folded her arms round herself, and began to walk away from him.

One foot in front of the other.

She could do this. She was strong. She'd survived worse emotional trauma in the past.

But, oh, this hurt. A deep, visceral pain of rejection.

You need time to think. I'll give you that.

The words echoed in Ben's head, over and over again.

Toni was walking away from him, just as Karen had. Except it wasn't the same thing at all. Karen had walked away because she'd fallen in love with his best friend; Toni was walking away because he'd pushed her away.

That wasn't what he wanted.

At all.

But it felt as if the beach had turned into set concrete, and he was stuck there. Worse still, it was as if someone had superglued his lips together. He couldn't open his mouth to call out to her, to ask her to wait. All he could do was watch her walking quickly away. And he hated himself for it.

Time seemed to stop.

Eventually he made a decision. He couldn't stay here. He needed to get away and think. To go home to London and take stock.

He took his phone from his pocket and called Ranjit. The head of the practice was sympathetic, and promised to sort out a locum to cover Ben's absence.

His next call was to his sister.

'I'm heading out to my aerobics class,' she said, 'but I'll be back by the time you get here. Of course you can stay. Stay as long as you like.' She paused. 'What's happened?'

'Tell you when I see you,' Ben said.

'OK. Drive safely.'

'I will,' he promised.

He drove home and packed a bag.

And then, just before he left, he texted Toni.

Sorry. I'm going back to London. I'll call you.

Once he'd got his head straight. He felt bad about hurting her, but he needed to think, and he couldn't do that here.

* * *

Selfish, stubborn and stupid.

That was Ben Mitchell.

How could he think that it was history re-peating itself? How?

Toni wanted to grab his shoulders and shake him until his teeth rattled. Though she knew it wouldn't make him any more likely to talk to her.

And the text he'd just sent her made her even angrier. Sorry? If he was really sorry, he wouldn't be walking away from her in the first place. He wouldn't be going back to London. And he certainly wouldn't be vague. *I'll call you*. When? This year, next year, sometime, never?

What was very clear was that she'd been very wrong indeed about Ben Mitchell and commitment. He didn't want to commit to her and their baby. Yet again, she'd picked Mr Wrong.

'You selfish, stubborn, *stupid* man,' she said through gritted teeth, and Archie woofed softly as if in agreement.

On the way back to London, Ben's phone rang; the display on the car's hands-free sys-tem told him it was his sister. Thinking she was probably wanting to know what time he was likely to arrive, he answered, 'Hi, Jessie.'

'Ben.' Her voice was high and breezy with panic. 'Are you still coming? It's Josh. He—he—he's in hospital.'

'Hospital?' Ben repeated, shocked. 'What's happened?'

'Kit gave him his dinner and then he just went red and stopped breathing. Kit called the ambulance and gave him CPR. The paramedic said it was anaphylactic shock. Oh, God, Ben. What if he—if he…?' She couldn't get the word out.

He knew what was going through her head. What if baby Josh died? 'He's going to be fine,' he said reassuringly. 'Many, many more infants survive anaphylaxis than die from it. Plus he's in hospital, so he's in the right place if there's another emergency. I know it's frightening, but I promise you the stats are all on your side. I'm about half-way to London now—tell me which hospital you're in and I'll let you know when I'm close.'

Her words were barely coherent but he worked out that she was at Muswell Hill Memorial Hospital.

'I'll be there soon. Is Kelly with you?'

'No. Kit's mum met us at the hospital and took her home.'

'That's good. And Kit's with you?'

'Yes. He came in the ambulance with Josh and Kelly. Oh, God, Ben, if I hadn't gone to aerobics tonight—'

'It would still have happened,' he told her gently. 'I'll be there soon. I love you and it's going to be fine, Jessie. I promise it's going to be fine.'

Anaphylactic shock. That meant Josh had a severe allergy to something. It had happened after Kit gave him his dinner, so the most likely culprits were nuts, milk, eggs or shellfish. And Ben could give his sister and brother-in-law all kinds of advice to help them keep Josh safe in the future.

It felt as if it took for ever to get to London, but when the satnav said he was fifteen minutes away from the hospital he used the car's hands-free system to text Jessie that he was nearly there. Finally he parked the car and headed for the Emergency Department.

'My nephew, Josh Harford, was brought in with anaphylactic shock this evening. I've driven straight here from Norfolk. Can you tell me if he's still in your department, please?' Ben asked the receptionist.

She checked for him. 'He's just been moved to the children's ward,' she said, and directed him to the paediatric department.

That was a good sign: it meant the baby was out of immediate danger, though Josh would probably be kept in overnight for observation and maybe for most of the next day.

At the paediatric department, the reception team directed him to Josh's bedside.

He rounded the corner and saw them in the little bay: Jessie and Kit with their arms wrapped around each other, and their free hands clearly holding Josh's.

'How's Josh doing?' Ben asked. 'And how are you both holding up?'

'Oh, Ben.' Jessie dissolved into sobs and he held her close, resting one hand on Kit's shoulder for comfort and support.

'It was all my fault,' Kit said. 'I gave him scrambled egg for his dinner. I thought it'd be nice and soft because he's been teething, and... Oh, God. Then he went red round the mouth and his face started swelling up, and he was having trouble breathing.' Kit was shaking. 'Thank God that work sent me on that first aid course the other month. I rang

999 and, by the time I'd done that, he was unconscious and I had to give him CPR. I thought we were going to lose him. I thought our baby was going to die.' Kit dragged a hand through his hair. 'I'm never going to forgive myself.'

'You weren't to know that he was allergic,' Ben told him. 'I'm assuming the paramedics gave him an injection of adrenalin?'

'And an oxygen mask, and a drip,' Kit said.

'That was all to help him breathe and sort out his blood pressure,' Ben said, reassuring him. 'I'm guessing Josh is going to be in here overnight and possibly tomorrow for observation.'

'I think that's what they said,' Kit said. He raked his hand through his hair again. 'Nothing the nurses tell us stays in my head, and they're so busy I can't keep bothering them. I just see Josh there and it's like a fog. I don't know what to do.'

Reassurance, Ben thought. That was what they needed. Reassurance.

'You're going to be just fine, aren't you, Josh?' he said gently.

The baby was asleep, but Ben was happy with the figures he could see on the machine next to the bed. 'I know right now it feels like the end of the universe, but Josh is in the right place and you're all going to get through this. I know what all those figures mean on that machine and I promise you it's all good.'

He could see Jessie and Kit both visibly relax as he spoke. 'Sit down,' he said, 'and I'll talk you through everything.' He held their hands. 'Ask me to repeat anything I say if you can't remember. It's fine. And I'll write it all down for you in a minute,' he told them. 'OK. Egg is one of the big four foods that can cause severe allergic reactions in children. The very first time Josh ate something with egg in it, he might have had a milder reaction to it. Given the age he is, the red face and swelling could look like normal teething symptoms rather than an allergic reaction,' he said.

'But this time, when he ate the egg, his immune system recognised the allergen and overreacted big-time. Hence the rash, the swelling and the breathing difficulties. He'll be fine, and before he leaves here the team will give you an auto-injector with adrenalin that you'll need to keep with him all the time, and a written emergency plan so anyone who might be looking after him knows what to do if it happens again.'

'Oh, my God. Are you telling me this could happen again?' Jessie asked, looking terrified. 'He could stop breathing like that and his heart could stop again?'

'If he accidentally eats something containing the allergen, then yes, his system will overreact to it again,' Ben said. 'But if that does happen then you'll know exactly what to do. And you'll have the adrenalin to use straight away, so it won't be quite as scary. When you leave here, you'll be given an appointment with your GP or an allergy specialist, and they'll do some tests to confirm that Josh is allergic to eggs and to check his reaction to any other of the big allergens, too. And your GP can give you advice on how to help Josh avoid allergens in future.' He paused. 'Actually, I can do that. I've got leaflets I give to my patients. I'll print out some copies at your place tonight, so anyone who looks after Josh will have the information to hand, too.'

'I'm so scared, Ben,' Jessie said, her teeth chattering.

'Of course you are. It's terrifying, seeing your baby lying there with an oxygen mask.

But it's going to be all right. They know what's wrong and they know how to treat him. Josh isn't going to die. He's going to recover from this.' He looked at Kit. 'You're both going to have to be really strict about the food he eats, but he'll be fine. Anaphylaxis is seriously scary, and I can't imagine what a nightmare it must be to have to give your own baby CPR.'

'It…' Kit was shivering. 'I thought he'd die.'

'But you gave him CPR. You saved his life,' Ben said.

'You saved him, Kit,' Jessie echoed. 'If it wasn't for you, he would have died.'

'But I was the one who gave him the egg in the first place—the thing that made him nearly die.'

'You weren't to know. It could just have easily been me,' Jessie said.

'Or anyone else who looked after Josh. Your parents, mine, a family friend.' Ben looked at them. 'And I bet neither of you has eaten anything tonight.'

'I couldn't face anything,' Kit said.

'Me neither,' Jessie admitted. 'And I haven't put the sheets on the spare bed for you or—'

'It's fine,' Ben cut in gently. 'Josh is going

to get through this, but I'm guessing neither of you want to leave him for a second, so I'm going to go and get you both something to eat and a hot drink. No arguments. You need to keep your strength up so you can support Josh.' And each other, he thought.

When he got back from the canteen with sandwiches and hot drinks, Kit and Jessie were clinging together, watching their infant as he slept.

'I know neither of you normally takes sugar, but right now I think you need it,' Ben said, handing them in the drinks. 'Josh is doing just fine. I want you to eat and drink now. No arguments.' He tried for humour. 'Doctor's orders.'

They'd both lost the grey tinge of anxiety, he was glad to notice.

It took him two hours, but eventually he persuaded Jessie to let him drive her home. And she only agreed because Kit was staying with Josh and because Ben pointed out that at least one of them needed to get some decent sleep to support Josh when he was discharged next day.

Ben sorted out the spare room, making Jessie go and rest even though he suspected she wouldn't sleep very much. It took him a long time to get to sleep, too, because the way Kit and Jessie had been together in a crisis had really made Ben think about what he wanted from life. He wanted the same warmth and closeness and utter trust in each other—true love.

And he wanted it with the mother of his baby. The woman he'd treated incredibly badly because he'd let his past get in the way. Of course that text was innocent. She hadn't told him about it because Sean meant nothing to her any more. Ben knew he'd been incredibly stupid and hurtful, and he needed to make amends.

It was too late to call her now, but he'd call her tomorrow. Or, better still, he'd go back to Norfolk and have that conversation face to face. Because being here in a familiar bit of London, just round the corner from the place he'd called home for so long, had made him realise that this wasn't home any more.

Norfolk was home.

With Toni.

If she'd give him the chance to make it up to her.

The next morning, he drove Jessie to pick up Kelly from Kit's parents, then took them to the hospital to see Josh. The baby was sitting on his dad's lap, bright-eyed, and he gurgled with joy when he saw his mum— setting Jessie in tears again, but this time they were happy tears.

Finally, just after lunch, Josh was discharged, and Ben drove them all home. He stayed long enough to be sure they'd settled in and would call him if they had the slightest worry, then headed back to Norfolk.

Ben knew Toni would be at work. It wouldn't be fair to call her and have a conversation at the surgery, but he definitely needed to talk to her. To apologise.

In the end, he texted her.

Coming back from London. Please can we talk this evening?

She still hadn't replied by the time he was almost back in Great Crowmell and he stopped off at a shop to buy flowers.

He couldn't blame her for being angry with him. He hadn't been fair to her; he'd let her down when she'd needed him most.

Would she give him a chance to explain, or would he end up making everything worse?

In the end he drove straight to her house.

Her car was parked outside, and the windows were open, so he was pretty sure that she was home.

He rang the doorbell.

A couple of minutes later, she opened the door; she stared at him, but said nothing. And there was a world of hurt in her eyes.

'I'm sorry,' he said, and tried to give her the flowers.

She leaned against the doorjamb with her arms folded, refusing to accept them. 'You're sorry.' Her voice was completely neutral and he didn't have a clue what was in her head.

'I'm sorry for a lot of reasons. I'm sorry I hurt you, I'm sorry I wasn't supportive when I should've been, and I'm sorry I was such an idiot,' he said. 'I let the past get in my way, and I shouldn't have done.'

'Yes. Because I'm not Karen. I've never even *met* your best friend—ex-best friend, whatever you want to call him—let alone had a fling with him.'

'I know.' He took a deep breath. 'I'm ashamed of myself. I should have supported you properly. What you told me was a shock, but it must've been a shock to you as well.'

'Uh-huh.' She didn't move.

'Can I come in?' he asked. 'Please?'

'Yes,' she said. 'But, just so we're clear, giving me flowers isn't what I want. It's not about gifts and throwing money at a problem—that's the sort of thing that Sean would've done.'

'Sean.' He was going to have to admit to that, too.

She stood aside and let him walk into her kitchen. Archie was there, but he didn't rush up and bounce about, the way he usually would. He stayed in his bed, looking mournful, and Ben felt even more guilty.

'These aren't a proper apology,' he said. 'I bought them because I know you like flowers.' Sweet-smelling stocks, roses and gerbera; to his relief, this time she accepted the flowers, but she didn't put them in water. She placed them on the draining board, folded her arms and looked at him.

'The apology…' He blew out a breath. 'I hardly know where to start. I'm completely in the wrong.'

'Yes.'

She wasn't going to make this easy for him; then again, he didn't deserve it to be easy.

'I let my past get in the way,' he said again. 'And I don't understand why.'

'Because of Sean.'

She frowned. 'What about Sean?'

'He texted you.'

Her frown deepened. 'And you think a text equates to having a fling?'

'No, of course it doesn't. But I couldn't stop myself wondering why you didn't mention it to me.'

'Because there wasn't anything to mention.' She shook her head in what he guessed was a mixture of frustration and exasperation. 'Why didn't you ask me about it, if you were that worried?'

He squirmed. 'Because I thought I was being paranoid and ridiculous.'

'You *were* being paranoid and ridiculous.' She rolled her eyes. 'I have no idea why he texted me. His text asked me to call him and said he missed me, which is utter rubbish. I thought either he'd texted me by mistake, or he was trying to schmooze me, because maybe he needed a plus-one at some event to help boost his career and he thought I might help him out—and, by the way, if that'd been the case I would've said no. I texted him to say I assumed he'd messaged me by mistake, and he never replied.'

'Seeing as I'm being ridiculous and paranoid, I might as well say the rest of it.' He had nothing else to lose. 'Why would you still have his number in your phone?'

A muscle worked in her cheek. 'Because,' she said, 'I changed my phone a couple of months before I met you. The phone shop transferred all my data across for me, and something went wrong so they ended up duplicating all my contacts. They said it's something to do with the way numbers are stored on a phone and on a SIM card and they couldn't fix it. I'd just have to delete the numbers I didn't want any more. I must've deleted his number off one of them but not the other, so when the techies messed up my data it ended up back in the list. I meant to tidy everything up but it's one of those jobs I kept putting off.'

The explanation was simple and completely plausible, and Ben felt even worse. 'Sorry.'

'And now you can give me a good reason why I shouldn't ask you to leave.'

'Because I'm an idiot,' he said, 'and because I need you.' That wasn't enough. He owed her total honesty. 'This scares me stupid, Toni, but I love you. My world's a much better place with you in it. I should've told you that when you told me about the baby, instead of letting everything get in the way and stomping off to London. And I wanted to tell you last night when I got back from the hospital—'

'Hang on. Hospital?' she interrupted.

'Josh ended up in the emergency department. Kit gave him egg and it turns out he's allergic to them. He had anaphylaxis,' Ben explained.

She looked shocked. 'Is he all right now? How are Jessie and Kit?'

Typical Toni. He'd hurt her and she had every right to be furious with him, yet she was putting other people first. 'He's fine. He's home now. Jessie and Kit are a bit wobbly but they're getting there. I gave them the anaphylaxis leaflet from the surgery so they've got everything written down, and I said I'd go with them to Josh's appointment with the allergy team because it'll be a lot to take in.'

'I'm glad he's OK,' she said.

'I'm so sorry I hurt you,' he said. 'Can I rewind to yesterday and say what I should have said? What I want to say?'

She looked wary. 'OK. But I'm still reserving the right to throw you out.'

'Absolutely,' he said. 'The news was a huge shock, but I shouldn't have said what I did. I should've thanked you for being brave enough to tell me so soon, because I'm guessing you'd only just found out, too, and it was a huge shock to you as well. And I want to apologise again, just in case I say anything over the next few minutes that hurts you, because I'd never want to do that. What's important is *you*. Are you all right?'

Then her face crumpled and she started to cry. Archie rushed over to her, shoving his nose into her hand in a gesture of doggy comfort. And Ben took a risk—he closed the distance between them and wrapped his arms tightly round her, holding her close, until she'd stopped shaking. Then he wiped away her tears with the pad of his thumb. 'Tell me about the baby,' he said softly. 'How did you find out?'

'I couldn't face my coffee at breakfast and my breasts felt sore. And then I counted back and realised my last period was eight weeks ago.' She dragged in a breath. 'Wednesday was my morning off, and it's school holidays so we didn't have reading group. I drove to the city to buy a pregnancy test and did it in the loos at the library.'

So nobody locally would know or guess.

'I think… I think it must've happened the day Ginny died. When we…' She bit her lip. 'I can't remember if we used a condom.'

The first time, at his house, they had. But in the middle of the night, when he'd been curled round her in her bed… 'I can't remember, either,' he admitted. 'I just wanted to comfort you. The rest of it's a blur.'

'I know the baby wasn't planned. And I know this must be hard for you, because of what happened with your ex.'

'That was a totally different situation. And I know I let that get in the way, but I had time to think about it yesterday and realised what an idiot I was being.' He stroked her face. 'Have you had time to start coming to terms with it? Any idea about what you want to do? Because, whatever you want, whatever you need, I'll support you. No pressure. You're the one who's important here, Toni, and I'll be guided by you.'

'Thank you.' She swallowed hard. 'I want to keep the baby. I'm clear on that. But I know this is going to be hard for you.'

'What's harder,' he said, 'is knowing that I hurt you, and I promise I'll never do that again. I should've just asked you. Been honest with you about what was in my head.'

'I'd never cheat on you.'

'I know. And I'll do my best to give you everything you need. I'll support you through every step of your pregnancy. Every bit of morning sickness, every single antenatal appointment, and I'll be right by your side all the way. Even when you're in transition and you crush my hand and yell at me.'

To his relief, she gave him a wry smile. 'I'll hold you to that.'

'Good. We've got a lot of things to work out,' he said, 'but the important thing is that we work them out together.'

But was he saying that because he wanted to be with her—or was this all for the baby's sake? Toni wondered. Was he doing what he thought was the right thing, or doing what he really wanted to do?

There was a big difference, and she didn't want him to be with her out of duty. She wanted him to be there because he loved her.

'So what made you change your mind? Yesterday, you walked out on me. Today, you're back.'

'Yesterday, I was very stupid and I let my

past get in the way. Yesterday, I watched my sister and her husband at their baby's bedside after Josh had stopped breathing. I saw how much they were a team, how they were there for each other—and I realised that was what I want. A real partnership. Love and liking and respect, the whole lot all bundled in together. And I want it with you.'

Could she believe him?

'What do you want, Toni?' he asked.

He'd asked her straight out, so she'd be honest with him in return. This might turn messy, but at least they'd both know exactly where they stood. It might be painful, but better that than quietly wishing and hoping and watching things turn pear-shaped because she hadn't had the courage to speak out when she should've done. And she never wanted to go through the misery of yesterday again.

'I want,' she said, 'to live with someone who loves me and who loves our baby. Someone who wants to be a family with me.' She looked him straight in the eye. 'What do *you* want, Ben?'

'I want to be a dad to our baby,' he said. 'And I want to be with you. Be a family with you. I want to make a future with you and our baby, if you'll have me. I'm not perfect and I'm going to get things wrong in the future. I'll do and say the wrong thing sometimes. But I'll never deliberately hurt you. And I'll do my best to talk to you instead of hiding away in my head. I'm scared that I won't be enough for you—like I wasn't for Karen, otherwise she wouldn't have fallen for Patrick. I know that makes me paranoid and ridiculous, but I owe you total honesty.'

'I thought you'd gone away because you didn't want commitment. I thought I'd picked another Mr Wrong.'

'Mr Wrong-headed, perhaps,' he said. 'But I do want commitment. I want everything, Toni, and I want it with you. If I'm enough for you.'

'You're enough for me,' she said. 'Just for the record, I wasn't expecting to fall in love with you. I didn't even like you, the first day I met you. I thought you were unreasonable and grumpy, and I was prepared to ignore you as much as I could.'

'I wasn't expecting to fall in love with you, either. You have one hell of a glare,' Ben said. 'And you refused my brownies.'

'I hate chocolate cake. Even posh, award-winning, super-special Viennese chocolate cake,' she said.

He smiled. 'But you tried it anyway because I asked you to.'

'You danced with me without complaining that I hurt your toes.'

'You didn't hurt my toes. You're perfectly capable of dancing, whether it's a waltz or a jitterbug.' He grinned. 'As long as you're being led by someone who knows what they're doing.'

'Like you.'

He stroked her face. 'Teamwork. We're good together, Toni, at work and outside. And all I could think about on the way back from London was you. I don't belong in London any more; I belong here, with you and our baby and Archie. This is where my life is. Where I want to be. You want commitment? You've got it. Because I love you, Toni Butler. I love everything about you and my world's a better place with you at its centre. And I really want to marry you. Not because of the baby, because of you.'

He loved her.

Just the way that she loved him.

This time, she'd found the right man. One who wasn't going to let her down or give her ultimatums. One who'd actually commit to her.

'I probably should ask you somewhere a lot more romantic. I maybe should've asked you in Vienna, in the middle of all the butterflies—because that's when I realised how much you make my world feel full of colour,' Ben said. 'But I want to be a family with you and Archie. I want to make sandcastles with our children and look for shells. I want to run on the beach with our dog at sunrise, and treat our patients, and be a proper part of this community. I want it all, and I want it with you. Will you marry me, Toni? Be my love, my life?'

'What do you think, Arch? Should we say yes?' she asked.

The dog gave a single woof.

'I agree,' she said with a smile. 'I love you, too, Ben. Yes.'

EPILOGUE

Ten months later

BEN STOOD IN the porch of the huge flint-built church at Great Crowmell with Toni at his side; he was carrying their daughter, Elizabeth, while she was carrying their son, Max. The twins were fast asleep; the godparents—Jessie, Kit, Stacey and Nick—were waiting inside with his parents, toddler Josh and a host of their friends. Archie had special dispensation to be at the christening, just as he had at the wedding, and was sitting under the watchful eye of Kelly.

'You're beautiful, Mrs Mitchell, and I love you very much,' he said, stealing a kiss. 'Are you ready for this?'

'Ready.' She smiled at him. 'Let's go and join our family and friends. And then we can get this party started...'

* * * * *

If you enjoyed this story, check out these other great reads from Kate Hardy

Heart Surgeon, Prince...Husband!
Carrying the Single Dad's Baby
Unlocking the Italian Doc's Heart
Their Pregnancy Gift

All available now!